OXFORD PROGRESSIVE ENGLISH READERS

General Editor: D. H. Howe

A Night of Terror and Other Strange Tales

Antique

A Night of Terror
and Other Strange Tales

黄志堅. Tony Wong

by GUY de MAUPASSANT

Translated and adapted by ARNOLD KELLETT

HONG KONG
OXFORD UNIVERSITY PRESS 1976
KUALA LUMPUR SINGAPORE JAKARTA TOKYO

Oxford University Press
OXFORD LONDON GLASGOW NEW YORK
TORONTO MELBOURNE WELLINGTON CAPE TOWN
IBADAN NAIROBI DAR ES SALAAM LUSAKA ADDIS ABABA
KUALA LUMPUR SINGAPORE JAKARTA HONG KONG TOKYO
DELHI BOMBAY CALCUTTA MADRAS KARACHI

ISBN 0 19 580748 0

Retold by A. Kellett. Illustrated by P. Kearney. Simplified according to the language grading scheme especially compiled by D.H. Howe

Also by Arnold Kellett:

Tales of Supernatural Terror
The Diary of a Madman and Other Tales of Horror
(unadapted translations of Maupassant, both published by Pan Books)

Printed by Sheck Wah Tong Printing Press, 653-657, King's Road, Hong Kong
Published by Oxford University Press, News Building, North Point, Hong Kong

Contents

Oxford Progressive English Readers Language Scheme

The OPER language grading scheme was especially compiled by D. H. Howe as a guide to the preparation of language teaching material for school pupils and adults learning English as a second or foreign language. The scheme provides lists of words and language structures subdivided into three grades of difficulty and meant to be used in conjunction with each other.

The items were chosen according to two main principles: first, that they are likely to have been learnt or at least encountered *before* the stage indicated; second, that they are frequently occurring and useful, necessary to express a wide range of ideas, and difficult to replace with simpler words or constructions.

Use of the scheme is intended to eliminate unnecessary difficulties of language which would otherwise hinder understanding and enjoyment.

Introduction

Guy de Maupassant is one of the most famous of French writers and well known in Europe for his short stories. He was born in 1850 in Normandy in the north of France. As a boy he mixed freely with country people and fishermen whom he later wrote about in his stories. After leaving school in Rouen he went to Paris to study law, but in 1870, when the Prussians attacked France, he joined the army. Although he hated army life he used his experiences as a soldier in his writing.

After the war he worked in government offices in Paris. He did not enjoy this life either, but it gave him more ideas for his short stories. After receiving help and advice from the famous author, Gustave Flaubert, he became a full-time writer. Soon he was very successful and made enough money to travel to places such as Corsica and North Africa.

Maupassant wrote about three hundred short stories. Most of them are about ordinary, everyday life, but he also wrote about mysterious events which fill men with terror. As a young man Maupassant picked up a disease which later affected his brain. At the age of 41 he became mad and, like the man in the story *Who knows?*, he spent the rest of his short life in a mental hospital.

1 A Night of Terror

As you ask me to tell you a few of my experiences on the river, I'll tell you about a strange thing that happened to me here about ten years ago.

One evening I was coming back home, feeling rather tired, and rowing with some difficulty my heavy boat, the twelve-foot boat which I always use at night-time. I stopped for a few moments to get my breath back, just over there. The weather was magnificent. The moon was shining brightly. The surface of the river was gleaming in the moonlight, and the air was still and mild. This peaceful scenery tempted me. I thought to myself that it would be very pleasant to stop here and smoke a pipe of tobacco. Without hesitation I picked up my anchor and threw it over the side.

The boat, which was being pulled down the river by the current, slipped to the end of the anchor-chain, then stopped. I sat down in the boat on a sheep-skin and made myself as comfortable as I could. There was not a sound to be heard, not a sound – except that occasionally I could just hear water moving against the river-bank. I could see tall grass rising above the bank, taking on strange shapes and swaying very slightly.

The river was absolutely calm, and yet I felt disturbed by the extraordinary silence which surrounded me. Even the frogs, creatures which normally make music at night, were not making a sound. Then, suddenly, somewhere to my right, a frog croaked*. The noise made me jump. It didn't croak again. I could hear nothing else, so I decided to smoke a little, just to give myself something to do.

But, you know, though I've smoked a pipe for many years, I just couldn't do it. After a few moments I felt sick, and so I stopped smoking. I started to sing a tune to myself, but the

**croak*, noise made by a frog.

sound of my voice somehow disturbed me, and so I lay down in the bottom of the boat and looked up at the sky.

I start feeling nervous

For a while I felt calm, but soon I became worried by the way the boat swayed from side to side. I felt as though it was swinging violently across the river, first touching one bank, then swinging across to the other. Then I felt that some creature or force, which I could not see, was gently pulling the boat to the bottom of the river, then lifting it up and letting it fall again. I imagined I was in the middle of a storm, and I could hear strange noises all round me. I leapt to my feet. The water was gleaming in the moonlight, and everything was calm.

I realized that I was suffering from nervousness, and I decided that it was time to move on. I pulled at my chain. The boat started to go towards it, and then I felt a resistance. I pulled harder, but the anchor wouldn't move. It had caught on something on the bottom of the river and I could not pull it up. I started pulling hard again, but it was no use.

Then, by using the oars, I turned the boat round and changed the position of the anchor. It was no good. It held as firmly as ever. I lost my temper and shook the chain angrily, but it still would not move even a tiny bit.

Very discouraged, I sat down and began to think about the mess I was in. I couldn't possibly break this chain or separate it from the boat. It was enormously thick and nailed to a piece of wood that was thicker than my arm. But as the weather was still very good, I thought it would not be long before some fisherman would come to my rescue.

This annoying discovery had calmed my nerves. I found that at last I was able to smoke my pipe. I had a bottle of rum* with me. I drank two or three glasses, and began to laugh at the situation I was in. The weather was really very mild, so if necessary I could spend the night in the open without coming to much harm.

**rum,* a strong drink made from sugar.

Suddenly there was the sound of a knock against the side of my boat. I jumped to my feet, and a cold sweat broke out all over my body. The sound had probably been made by a piece of wood carried along by the current, but it had been enough to upset me. Once again I felt myself held by a strange nervousness. I seized the anchor-chain and pulled on it as hard as I could in one final desperate effort. The anchor held firm. I sat down again, tired out.

The mist

Meanwhile the river had gradually become covered with a very thick, white mist which crept along close to the surface of the water. When I stood up I could no longer see either the river or my feet, or the boat. It was as though I was buried up to my waist in a sheet of brilliantly white cotton-wool. I began to think of all kinds of strange things. I imagined that somebody was trying to get into the boat, which I could no longer see beneath me, and that the river, hidden by this thick fog, must be full of mysterious creatures which were swimming all round me.

I experienced a nasty feeling of weakness, as though I was going to faint. My heart was beating so hard that I seemed to be short of breath. I seriously thought of jumping into the river and swimming to safety. Then, immediately, this idea made me tremble with fright. I pictured myself lost in this thick mist, struggling amongst the water-weeds, breathing hard in terror, unable to see the river-bank, unable to find my boat. I seemed to feel myself being dragged down by my feet into the depths of that black water.

In fact, I would have had to swim against the current for at least five hundred yards before finding a part free from water-weeds, where I could get a proper foot-hold. I had a ninety per cent chance of losing my way in the fog and of getting drowned, even though I was a very good swimmer.

My stupid fear, impossible to explain, was still increasing and was now becoming real terror. I stood there without moving, with my eyes open wide and my ears listening for the slightest sound. I think that if a fish had suddenly decided to jump out of the water, as fish frequently do, that would have been quite enough to make me fall flat on my face, unconscious.

However, by trying to control myself I managed to bring my state of mind gradually back to normal. Once again I took my bottle of rum and drank from it greedily. Then I had an idea. I started to call out at the top of my voice, facing in turn north, south, east and west. When my throat hurt so much that I couldn't shout any more, I stood and listened. All I could hear was the distant howling of a dog.

I drank some more rum, then I lay down, stretching myself at full length along the bottom of the boat. I stayed like this for perhaps an hour – possibly two hours – without going to sleep, with my eyes wide open. I didn't dare sit up and yet I very much wanted to do so. Each minute I kept putting it off, saying to myself, 'Come on, sit up!' But I was too afraid to move. At last I slowly began to raise myself, taking extreme care as I did so, as if my very life depended on the slightest sound I might make. I looked over the side of the boat.

A scene from fairyland

I saw the most wonderful, the most amazing sight it is possible to imagine. It was just like a scene from fairyland, one of those scenes which travellers from distant countries describe to us, and we listen without really believing them. The fog, which two hours before had been hanging over the water, had gradually lifted and settled over the banks. Leaving the river entirely clear, it had formed on each side a long, continuous hill, which shone in the moonlight with the splendid brightness of snow. Overhead a full, brilliant moon was set in a sky of milky blue.

All the inhabitants of the river-bank had now come to life and the frogs were croaking loudly. Curiously enough I was no longer afraid. I was surrounded by such extraordinary scenery that the strangest events would not have surprised me in the least.

I have no idea how long this lasted because I fell asleep. When I opened my eyes again, the moon had gone down and the sky was full of clouds. The water was splashing sadly against the boat. The wind was blowing. It was cold and completely dark.

I drank what was left of the rum, then, as I sat there shivering*, I listened to the strange threatening sound made by the current. I could not see my boat, nor even my hands when I held them close to my eyes.

Help arrives at last

Gradually, however, it grew less dark. Suddenly I thought I sensed a dark shape moving along, quite near to me. I gave a shout, and a voice answered me. It was a fisherman. I called across to him and he rowed up to me. I told him all about my misadventure. He brought his boat alongside mine, and together we pulled on my anchor-chain. The anchor still would not move.

The day was dawning. It was a grey, wet, cold sort of day, one of those days which you feel sure is going to bring you sorrow and misfortune. I noticed another boat, and we shouted across to it. The man who was in it rowed up and helped us. Finally, little by little, the anchor began to move. It came up very, very slowly, and was evidently carrying a considerable weight. At last we saw a great black lump coming out of the water, and we dragged it into my boat.

It was the body of an old woman, with a huge stone tied round her neck.

**shivering,* trembling with cold.

2 The Hand

They had gathered in a circle round Mr Bermutier, the judge, who was giving his opinion of a mysterious crime. Everybody in Paris was talking about it but nobody could solve the mystery. Standing with his back to the fire-place, Mr Bermutier was talking away, discussing various explanations, but not reaching any decision.

Several women had got up and drawn nearer. They stood round him, excited by that combination of fear and curiosity, that eager demand for terror, which possesses the minds of women and becomes a kind of hunger.

There was a moment of silence. Then one of them, paler than the others, said, 'It's frightening! It seems like something supernatural*. We shall never solve it.'

The judge turned towards her.

'Yes, madam. We probably never shall get to the bottom of it. But as for this word "supernatural" that you've used, it doesn't apply in this case. We are dealing with a crime which was so cleverly thought out, and so cleverly carried out, that we cannot explain it. But I once had to deal with a case which really *did* seem to have something supernatural about it. We had to abandon it, as a matter of fact, because there was simply no way of clearing it up.'

Several of the women suddenly called out, all at the same time, 'Oh, do tell us about it!'

Mr Bermutier smiled the serious smile which is suitable for a judge, and began his story.

The judge's story

'Now, you mustn't imagine for a moment that I give a supernatural explanation to anything in this story myself. It would be much better if we simply said that we could not find an explanation, instead of using the word "supernatural"

**supernatural,* beyond the laws of science, something that cannot be explained.

to describe what we do not understand. However, here are the facts:

'At that time I was working in Ajaccio, a little white town in a wonderful bay in the island of Corsica, surrounded on all sides by high mountains.

'My special job there was to deal with vendettas. A vendetta is the terrible custom which forces a man who has been wronged to take revenge on the man who has wronged him, and on his descendents and relations. I have seen old men, children, cousins – all murdered. I used to have my mind filled with events of this kind.

'Now, one day I heard that an Englishman had just rented a small house at the far end of the bay. He had brought with him a servant who was a Frenchman.

'Soon everybody was taking an interest in this strange person, who lived alone and never went out except to go hunting and fishing. He never spoke to anybody, never came into town, and every morning he would spend an hour or two in shooting-practice with pistol and rifle.

'Stories began to grow round him. It was claimed that he was a person of some importance who had run away from his own country for political reasons. Then people said that he was hiding because he had committed some dreadful crime. They even supplied particularly terrible details.

'In my official position I tried to obtain some information about this man, but I found it impossible to learn anything except that he called himself Sir John Rowell.

'So I had to remain content with keeping a close watch on him though, in fact, I had never received reports of anything suspicious about him.

'However, as the stories grew worse and began to spread, I made up my mind to see this stranger for myself, and I started to go shooting in the district where he lived.

The judge meets Sir John

'It was a long time before I had my opportunity, but at last I shot and killed a bird quite close to his house. My dog brought the bird to me, but I took it immediately to Sir John Rowell and asked him to accept it. At the same time I said I was sorry if I had disturbed him with my shooting.

'He was a big man, with red hair and a red beard. He was tall and had broad shoulders. He seemed like a calm giant, with very good manners. He thanked me very much for being polite enough to offer him the bird. During the following month we talked together five or six times.

'Then one evening, as I was passing his gate, I saw him smoking his pipe, sitting on a chair in the garden. I greeted him, and he invited me into the garden for a drink. I didn't need asking twice!

'I began to ask about his past life and about his plans for the future. He told me that he had travelled a good deal in Africa, India and America. He then said, with a laugh, "I've had plenty of adventures. I have indeed!"

'He began to tell me all sorts of interesting things about the hunting of tigers, elephants and other fierce animals.

' "Those are all awful monsters," I said.

' "Oh, no!" he said, with a smile. "The worst monster of all is man!" And he gave a loud laugh, then said, "I've often hunted man, too."

'Then he began to talk about guns, and he invited me to come into the house and see the various kinds of rifles he had. The walls of his room were covered in black silk on which were big golden flowers.

The dead hand

'In the middle of the wall a strange object attracted my attention. It was black and stood out clearly against a square of red silk. I went up to it. It was a hand, a human hand – not just the bones, all white and clean, but a black, dried hand, with yellow finger-nails. I could see the muscles and patches of dried blood, looking like dirt. The hand had been chopped off at about the middle of the arm, and it looked as though it had been done with an axe.

'An enormous iron chain was fixed to this dreadful limb,

and at the other end it was attached to the wall by a ring strong enough to hold an elephant.

'I asked him, "What's that?"

'The Englishman replied calmly, "That's my worst enemy. It came from America. It was chopped off with a sword, then the skin was taken off with a sharp bit of stone and it was dried in the sun for a week. It was a job well done, too."

'I touched the human hand. It must have belonged to a giant. The fingers were unusually long and were held in place by muscles which still had bits of skin sticking to them. This hand was a frightening thing to see. You could not help thinking that it was the result of some cruel act of revenge.

'"This man must have been very strong," I remarked.

'The Englishman replied in a gentle voice, "Oh yes. But I was stronger than he was. I fixed that chain on his hand to prevent it from escaping."

'I thought he must be joking, so I said, "That chain won't be much use now. The hand won't run away!"

'Sir John Rowell then said in a very serious voice, "It's *always* trying to get away. That chain is necessary."

'I took a quick glance at his face, saying to myself, "Is he mad, or is this a joke?"

'But the expression on his face remained calm, so I changed the subject and began to admire his guns.

'I noticed, however, that three loaded pistols had been placed on various pieces of furniture, as though this man lived in constant fear of being attacked.

'I made several more visits to his home, and then I stopped going there. We had become accustomed to his presence and people now paid little attention to him.

Sir John is murdered

'A whole year went by. Then one morning towards the end of November, my servant woke me with the news that Sir John Rowell had been murdered during the night.

'Half an hour later I was entering the Englishman's house with the captain of police. Sir John's servant, in despair and crying, was standing at the door. At first I suspected this man, but he turned out to be innocent. We never did discover who the murderer was.

'When I entered the room the first thing I saw was the body lying on its back in the middle of the floor.

'Sir John's waistcoat and a sleeve of his jacket had been torn. Everything suggested that a terrible struggle had taken place.

'The Englishman had been choked to death. His face was black and swollen, a terrible sight. The expression on his face suggested that he had experienced the most dreadful horror. He was holding something between his teeth, and in his neck, which was covered with blood, there were five holes. They looked as though they had been made by sharp points of iron.

'A doctor arrived. He spent a long time examining the

marks of the fingers in the flesh, and then said, "You'd think he'd been choked to death by fingers of bone!"

The hand had disappeared

'I suddenly felt cold run down my back, and immediately I looked at the place on the wall where earlier I had seen that terrible hand. It was no longer there. The chain had been broken, and was hanging down.

'Then I bent over the body. In the twisted mouth I found one of the fingers of the missing hand. It had been cut off, or rather bitten off, by the dead man's teeth.

'We continued with our search but we could discover nothing. No door or window had been forced open, and nothing had been broken into. The two guard dogs had not even wakened.

'The servant told us that for the past month his master had seemed very upset. He had received a lot of letters which he had burnt as soon as they arrived. Often he had picked up a whip and in a terrible temper which seemed almost like madness, he had fiercely beaten the dried hand which had somehow been removed at the time the crime took place. Sir John used to go to bed very late, and he carefully locked all the doors and windows. He always kept guns within easy reach. Often, at night, the servant had heard him talking in a loud voice, as though he were quarrelling with someone.

'On that particular night he had not made a sound, and it was only when he came to open the windows the next morning that the servant had found Sir John lying there, murdered.

'I told the police everything I knew about the dead man, and they made the most careful search over the whole island. Nothing was discovered.

'Now, one night, three months after the murder, I had a terrible dream. I thought I saw the hand, that dreadful hand, running like a spider all over the curtains and walls of my room. Three times I woke up, three times I fell asleep again, three times I saw that ugly human hand crawling rapidly round my bedroom, using its fingers as a creature uses its legs.

'In the morning the hand was brought to me. They had found it lying on Sir John's grave. The first finger was missing.

'Well, ladies. There's my story. That's all I know.'

The judge's explanation

The women who had been listening to the judge were filled with horror, and looked pale and trembling. One of them said, 'But that's not a proper ending! You haven't given us an explanation. We shall not be able to get to sleep tonight unless you tell us your opinion of what really happened.'

The judge gave his serious smile. 'Oh, ladies. I'm afraid I am going to prevent you from having terrible nightmares* about this! I simply think that the true owner of the hand was still alive. I think he came back to get the hand that had been chopped off, and that he managed it by using the one good hand that remained. The only thing is, I just haven't been able to find out how he did it. It must have been a sort of vendetta.'

One of the women muttered, 'No. That can't be the real explanation.' And the judge, still smiling, finally remarked, 'Well, I told you that my explanation wouldn't satisfy you!'

**nightmare,* a dream full of terror.

3 A Coward

Everybody called him 'Signoles', but he liked to use his full name – Viscount Joseph de Signoles. His parents had both died, leaving him a good deal of money. He was quite handsome, spoke well, and looked very noble and proud. All the ladies liked him, and he lived a peaceful, completely happy life.

He was supposed to be very good with a sword and even better with a pistol*.

'If I have to fight a duel* with anybody,' he used to say, 'I shall choose a pistol. If I use that weapon I shall be absolutely certain of killing my enemy.'

Now, one evening, he had been to the theatre with two ladies and their husbands. Afterwards he had invited them into a restaurant and bought them ice-cream. They had been there a few minutes when he noticed that a man sitting at a table nearby was staring at one of the two ladies. She seemed upset, annoyed, and she turned her head away from the man who was staring at her. Finally she said to her husband, 'There's a man over there who won't take his eyes off me. I don't know him at all. Do *you* know him?'

Her husband, who had not really noticed anything, looked at the man and remarked, 'No. I've never seen him before.'

The young woman, half smiling and half in anger, said, 'Well, it's very annoying. That man is spoiling my ice-cream.'

'Oh, don't take any notice of him,' said her husband. 'If we spent time on all the people who behave rudely we'd never finish!'

But Signoles had suddenly jumped to his feet. He could not bear the thought that a stranger should spoil an ice-cream that he had bought for a lady. He felt that he was the one

**pistol,* a small hand-gun.
**duel,* a fight between two people.

who had been insulted because it was he who had invited his friends into the restaurant.

He went up to the stranger and said, 'Sir, I cannot bear the way you are staring at these ladies. Please stop it!'

'Go away!' said the man.

'Take care, sir!' said Signoles angrily. 'You are going to make me forget myself!'

The man simply replied by saying one word, a rude word which could be heard all over the restaurant and which came as a shock to every person sitting there. They all made a sudden movement as though they had been moved by a spring. Everybody turned to look.

The duel is arranged

For a moment there was absolute silence, then suddenly, a sharp sound. Signoles had struck the man across the face. People stood up to stop the fight. The two men exchanged visiting cards. They would fight a duel.

When Signoles got home he walked up and down his room for a few minutes. He was too upset to think properly. Only one idea filled his mind: 'A duel!' He had done what he should have done. People would talk about him now. They would say he had done the honourable thing. They would speak well of him.

'What a pig that man is!' he said aloud.

Then he sat down and began to think. Early the next morning he would have to find some seconds – two friends who would help to arrange the duel. Who would he choose? He thought about the richest and most famous of his friends. Finally he decided to ask a nobleman and an army officer whose names would look well in the newspapers.

He noticed that he was thirsty and drank three glasses of water, one after the other. Then he started to walk up and down the room again. He decided that he would be brave. He would ask for a serious duel – one which would lead to death. Perhaps if he did this his enemy would not want to fight a duel, after all. Perhaps he would find an excuse.

He picked up the stranger's visiting card which he had thrown on the table. He had glanced at it in the restaurant and on the way back, and now he read it again. It simply said, 'George Lamil, 51 Moncey Street.'

He stared at these mysterious words. George Lamil! Who was this man? What kind of work did he do? Why had he looked at this woman in this way? How disgusting it was that a complete stranger should suddenly come and upset your life, just because he had felt like staring at a woman.

'What a pig!' said Signoles once again.

Then he stood still. He kept on staring at the card, feeling anger and hatred growing inside him. How silly the whole business was! He took a pen-knife and stuck it into the name printed on the card, just as if he was sticking a sword into a real person.

So he would have to fight! Should he choose a sword or a pistol? He considered that he was the person insulted, and so he had a right to choose the weapon to be used. With a sword there was less risk of being killed. But if he chose a pistol there was a chance that his enemy might not want to fight. There certainly was a serious risk of being killed if they used pistols, but it was worth taking the risk, because the other man might be too afraid to go ahead with the duel, and then people would say that he, Signoles, had behaved in an honourable way.

'I must be firm,' he said. 'He'll be too afraid to fight.'

The sound of his voice made him tremble, and he looked round the room feeling very nervous. He drank another glass of water and started to get undressed.

Signoles is too frightened to sleep

As soon as he got into bed he blew out the candle and closed his eyes.

'I have all day tomorrow to think about this,' he said. 'I'll have a good night's sleep. I'll be all right in the morning.'

He felt quite warm between the sheets, but he could not get to sleep. He turned over and over in bed, lying for five minutes on his back, then on his left side, then on his right side.

He was still thirsty. He got up to have another drink of water. Then he was suddenly filled with a terrible anxiety.

'What's the matter with me? Could it be that I'm afraid?'

Why did his heart start to beat madly at each little sound in the room? When the clock was going to strike, the sound caused by the spring made him jump and made him so nervous that he had to breathe with his mouth open for a few seconds.

'Is it possible,' he asked aloud, 'to be afraid in spite of yourself?'

And he began to be filled with doubt and terror. What would happen if a power stronger than his will took hold of him? Yes, what would happen then? He would, of course, go to fight the duel, because he wanted to. But what if he started trembling? What if he fainted? And he began to think about the mess he was in, about his reputation, about his good name.

Suddenly he was seized by a peculiar need to get up again and look at himself in the mirror. He lit his candle. When he saw his face reflected in the glass of the mirror he hardly recognised himself. It seemed as though he had never seen himself before. His eyes looked enormous, and he was pale. My word! How pale he was!

Signoles thinks about his own death

He stood looking at himself in the mirror. He put out his tongue to see if it looked healthy. Then suddenly, this thought entered his brain: 'By this time tomorrow I might be dead!'

And his heart started to beat violently.

'By this time tomorrow I might be dead. This person in front of me, this *me* that I see in the mirror, will not exist any more! Here I am. I can see myself. I know I am alive, and in twenty-four hours I shall be lying in that bed, dead, with my eyes closed, cold, stiff, gone for ever!'

He turned round and looked at the bed. He could clearly picture himself lying on his back in the very sheets he had just left. He had the hollow face of a dead man, and soft hands that would never move again.

Now he was afraid to go back to bed. He went into the next room and started to smoke a cigar. He felt cold. He was going towards the bell, ready to ring to wake up his servant. But he stopped, and said, 'If I call my servant he'll notice that I'm afraid.'

He did not ring. He lit a fire himself, with trembling hands. His thoughts were becoming confused. He felt as though he was drunk. He kept on saying to himself, 'What am I going to do? What's going to become of me?'

His whole body was trembling, shaking all over. He got up and went to the window to open the curtains.

Day was dawning, a summer's day. The sky was pink and was making all the roofs and walls look pink. The world was waking up to this great shower of bright light, coming down like a kiss from the rising sun. As soon as he saw the cheerful brightness his heart was filled with hope. How crazy he was to let himself be made miserable by fear! Nothing was decided yet. His seconds had not yet seen those of George Lamil, and he didn't even know for certain that he would have to fight.

He got dressed and left the house, walking with a firm step. As he walked he kept on saying to himself, 'I must be strong, very strong. I must show people that I am not afraid.'

His two seconds, the nobleman and the officer, were waiting for him.

After they had both given him a warm hand-shake the officer asked him, 'Do you want a serious duel?'

'Very serious,' replied Signoles.

'Are you going to use a pistol?'

'Yes.'

'Can we go ahead and arrange everything?'

'Twenty yards,' said Signoles, speaking with a dry, nervous voice. 'On the command we take aim and fire. We keep on shooting until there is a serious wound.'

'Those are excellent conditions,' said the officer. 'You shoot well. All the luck is on your side.'

Signoles then went back home to wait until they had arranged everything. His nervousness, which had disappeared for a few minutes, was now getting worse and worse. He seemed to be trembling all down his legs and arms. He could not sit still. He could not stand still. His mouth was so dry that his tongue seemed stuck, and it made a peculiar sound when he moved it.

He thought he would have some lunch, but he could not eat anything. Then he had the idea that if he drank some rum it would give him courage. He drank six small glasses, one after the other.

A warm, burning feeling spread through his body, and his mind seemed to be filled with a kind of mist.

'This is the way to do it,' he thought. 'I shall be all right now.'

An hour later he had drunk the whole bottle of rum and he was in a terrible state. He felt as though he wanted to roll about on the floor, shouting and biting.

The seconds arrive

It was getting dark when the door-bell rang. The sound gave him such a shock that he hadn't the strength to stand up when his two seconds entered the room. He hardly dared speak even a single word to them, because he was afraid they would discover what state he was in by the sound of his voice.

'Everything has been arranged according to the conditions you suggested,' said the officer. 'Your enemy at first claimed that he was the one who had been insulted so he had a right to choose the weapons. But he gave in almost immediately. His seconds are both army officers.'

'Thank you,' said Signoles.

'We'll have to go now,' said the nobleman. 'We still have a lot to do. We need to get a good doctor, because the fight will only stop when there has been a serious wound. You can't play games with bullets, as you know. We must find a place near a house where we can carry the wounded man, if necessary. Anyhow, we'll be another two or three hours.'

'Thank you,' said Signoles a second time.

'Are you all right?' asked the officer. 'Are your nerves steady?'

'Yes. Very steady, thank you.'

And the two seconds left the house.

When he was all alone again he felt as though he was going to go mad. He sat down at his writing-desk and wrote at the top of a page: 'This is my last Will and Testament*. . . '

Then he jumped up and walked away from the desk, unable to think properly or to make any kind of decision, even a simple one.

So he was going to fight a duel! He could not avoid it now. What was happening inside him? He *wanted* to fight, he was very definite about that. And yet he knew that in spite of all his efforts he would not even be able to find the necessary strength to get to the place where the duel would be fought. He tried to imagine what it would look like. He pictured himself standing there, and he pictured his enemy facing him.

He tried to read, picking up a book about shooting. Then he thought, 'Is my enemy an expert with a pistol? How can I find out?' He remembered that he had a book which contained a list of all those who were famous for shooting. He looked carefully through it. The name George Lamil was not there. But if this man was not sure he could kill his enemy, why had he agreed to fight a duel which might lead to death?

He opened a box containing a pair of pistols. He took one of them out and held it, taking aim, as if he was ready to shoot. But his hand was trembling so much that he could not keep the gun steady. It was waving about, pointing in all directions.

'It's impossible!' he said. 'I can't fight a duel in this state!'

He looked at the end of the pistol and saw the little black hole which spits death. He thought of the disgrace. People would whisper about him. They would laugh at him. The

**Will and Testament,* a paper saying what is to be done with money and property after a person's death.

ladies would hate him. There would be things about him in the newspapers. Cowardly men would insult him.

He kept on staring at the weapon in his hand. Suddenly he noticed that the pistol was already loaded. This gave him a strange feeling of pleasure, which he could not explain. Everybody would expect him to face his enemy in a manner that was noble and calm. If he failed to do so life would not be worth living. Everyone would pour scorn on him. They would treat him as a man who had done something dreadful and shameful. He would no longer have any friends. And he knew very well that he would not have this calm, courageous manner when he stood in front of his enemy.

Signoles kills himself

Yet he *was* brave, after all. A thought flashed rapidly through his mind. He suddenly opened his mouth wide, pushed the pistol into it as far as it would go, then fired. . .

When his servant heard the bang he rushed into the room and found him lying on his back. Some blood had fallen on the white sheet of paper on the desk, and there was a great splash of red above the words: 'This is my last Will and Testament'.

4 The Inn

The Schwarenbach Inn is like all the other wooden houses in the bare valleys which cut into the white mountain-tops of the Alps.

For the six months of summer it remains open, with John Hauser's family there. Then, as soon as the early snows begin to gather, filling the valley and making the descent to Leuk difficult, the women and the father, with his three sons, go away and leave the house to be looked after by the old guide Gaspard Hari and his companion.

The two men, with their big mountain-dog, Sam, live in their prison of snow until the spring arrives. They have nothing to look at except the great white slopes of the Balmhorn, surrounded by pale glittering mountain-peaks. They are shut in, buried under the snow, which rises all round them, crushing the little house, piling up on the roof, covering the windows and walling up the door.

On the day on which the Hauser family left for Leuk, the winter was closing in, and the descent was becoming dangerous.

The three sons set off on foot, leading three donkeys loaded with clothes and luggage. Behind them came the mother, Jean Hauser, and her daughter Louise, riding a fourth donkey. Last came the father and the two caretakers who were to accompany the family as far as the beginning of the track that leads down the mountainside.

A flood of sunshine fell across this white desert of snow, lighting it up with a cold, blinding brightness. There was no sign of life in this ocean of mountains; not a movement could be seen, not a sound disturbed the deep silence.

Gradually, the young guide, Ulrich Kunsi, a tall Swiss, went ahead of Hauser and old Gaspard Hari, and reached the donkey on which the two women were riding.

The youngest daughter looked at him as he came up to her, and there was sadness in the glance with which she welcomed him. She was a little fair-haired country girl. Her hair was so pale that you might imagine it had been made white by staying so long amongst the snow and ice.

When he reached the donkey on which she was riding, he slowed down. Mother Hauser began to talk to him, explaining in great detail how they should spend the winter. It was the first time that Ulrich had stayed behind. Old Hari, on the other hand, had already spent fourteen winters under the snow that covered the Schwarenbach Inn.

Ulrich Kunsi listened, but without taking his eyes off the girl. Every now and then he would reply, 'Yes, Mrs Hauser.' But his thoughts seemed far away, and his face remained calm.

They reached the Daubensee Lake, whose surface, a level sheet of ice, lay at the bottom of the valley. Below them in an enormous hollow at the foot of terrifying steep slopes, they caught sight of Leuk, its houses looking like bits of sand. The donkeys stopped at the edge of the path which winds all down the mountainside until it reaches the almost unseen village at the foot.

The two women jumped down into the snow. The two old men had now caught up with them. 'Come along,' said old Hauser, 'we must say goodbye, and wish each other all the best till next year.'

Old Hari repeated, 'Till next year!' Mrs Hauser gave her cheeks to be kissed, and her daughter followed her example.

When it was Ulrich Kunsi's turn to kiss Louise, he whispered in her ear, 'Don't forget those of us who are up there.'

'No,' she replied, so quietly that he guessed, rather than heard, what she said.

'Come along. It's goodbye!' said Jean Hauser again. 'Take care of yourselves!'

And, going in front of the women, he led the way down.

They were out of sight as soon as they turned the first bend in the track.

The two men are left alone

The two men turned round and started back to the Schwarenbach Inn.

They walked slowly, side by side, without speaking. They had seen the last of their friends. They would be alone, just the two of them, for four or five months.

Gaspard Hari began to tell Ulrich about the winter before. His companion then had been Michael Canol, who was now too old for this job. An accident could easily happen during the long period of loneliness. Still, they had not been bored. The secret of the whole thing was to make up your own entertainment and games, and find things to pass the time.

Ulrich Kunsi listened to his companion, but his thoughts were following the women, who were making their way to the village down the winding path on the mountainside.

Soon they caught sight of the inn. It was so tiny it could only just be seen, a black dot at the base of the huge sweep of snow.

When they opened the door, Sam the great curly-haired dog, started to jump around them.

'Now then, Ulrich,' said old Gaspard, 'we've no women here now. We must make the dinner ourselves. You can get the potatoes ready.'

And sitting on wooden stools, they began to prepare the soup.

The morning of the following day seemed long to Ulrich Kunsi. Old Hari smoked his pipe and spat into the fireplace, whilst the younger man looked through the window at the brilliant mountain which rose in front of the house.

In the afternoon he went out, and following the route they had taken the day before, he followed the tracks of the donkey on which the two women had ridden. When he reached the edge he lay on his stomach to look down on the village below. Seen from this height, the low houses looked like stones set in a field.

The young Hauser girl was now in one of those grey houses. Which one was it? They were too far away for Ulrich Kunsi to make out. How he wished he could go down there, while it was still possible!

But the sun had disappeared behind the great mountain of Wildstrubel, and the young man went back. He found old Hari smoking. When he saw him enter, Hari suggested a game of cards, and the two men sat down on opposite sides of the table. They played for a long time, then they had supper and went to bed.

The days that followed were like the first, clear and cold, without any fresh fall of snow. Gaspard used to spend his afternoons watching the eagles and the few birds which come up to these frozen mountain tops. But Ulrich went regularly to look down at the village. In the evening they played cards and other games.

The first heavy snowfall

One morning Hari, who had been the first to get up, called out to Ulrich. A cloud of white snow, deep yet light, was coming down on them, settling all around them, silently and gradually burying them under a thick heavy covering. The snowfall lasted four days and nights.

They had to clear the doors and windows, dig a way out, and cut steps so they could climb out on to the surface of the ice.

After that they lived like prisoners, hardly ever daring to go outside their dwelling. The housework was shared between them. Ulrich Kunsi did the cleaning and washing and kept the house tidy. He also chopped the firewood whilst Hari did the cooking and kept the fire going. They never quarrelled. They never even showed bad temper, or spoke roughly to each other, both having made up their minds to make the best of their winter stay on the mountain-tops.

Occasionally old Gaspard took his gun and went out hunting mountain deer, and when he had the good luck to kill one it was a great day in the Schwarenbach Inn, and there was a feast of fresh meat.

One morning Hari set out on one of these expeditions. The

temperature outside the inn was eighteen degrees below zero. He had left before sunrise hoping to take the deer by surprise on the lower slopes of the Wildstrubel.

Left to himself, Ulrich remained in bed until ten o'clock. He was a good sleeper, but he would not have dared to stay in bed in the presence of the old guide, who was always full of energy and an early riser.

He took a long time over his breakfast, which he shared with Sam, who spent his days and nights sleeping in front of the fire. Then he began to feel somehow frightened by the loneliness.

Then he went out to meet his companion, who was due to return at four o'clock.

The deep valley was now completely level under its thick cover of snow. Beneath the enormous peaks, the valley was now one great basin of frozen, blinding whiteness.

It was three weeks since Ulrich had been to the edge from which he could look down at the village. He wanted to go there again, before climbing the slopes that led to the Wildstrubel. But the snow had now covered the village and the houses could scarcely be seen under their coat of white.

He strode along, driving his iron-pointed stick down into the snow, which was as hard as stone. With his sharp eyes he looked for the small black dot which he expected to see moving in the distance on this great sheet of snow.

On reaching the edge he stopped, wondering whether old Hari had really come that way. Then, with quicker steps and increasing anxiety, he went on.

The sun was sinking. The snow was coloured with shades of pink, and over its glittering surface swept a dry and icy wind. Ulrich called out with a long echoing shout. His voice seemed to take flight in the death-like silence of the sleepy mountain. It rang far out over the deep frozen waves of the sea. Then it died away. And there was no answer.

Ulrich gives up the search for Hari

He walked on. The sun had sunk behind the distant mountain-tops and the purple glow of sunset still remained above them. But the depths of the valley were becoming grey, and the young man suddenly felt afraid. He felt as though the silence, the cold, the loneliness, were taking possession of him, were about to freeze his blood, make his limbs go stiff and change him into a solid frozen object. As fast as he could, he ran back towards the inn. The old man, he thought, must have already got back home. He would have returned by a different route and he would find him sitting by the fire, with a dead mountain-deer at his feet.

He soon came in sight of the inn. There was no smoke rising from the chimney. Ulrich ran still faster, and opened the door. Sam leaped up to greet him, but Gaspard Hari had not returned.

Nervously Kunsi kept turning round, as though expecting to find his companion hiding in a corner. Then he lit the fire again and made the soup, hoping that he would soon see the old man coming in.

From time to time he went outside to see if there was any sign of him. Night had fallen, the pale night of the mountains, lit up only by the thin, yellow shape of a new moon, which was low on the horizon and would soon be sinking behind the mountain-tops.

Returning to the house the young man sat down by the fire, and while he was warming his hands and feet he began to think of the accidents which might have happened. Gaspard might have broken a leg, or fallen into a deep hole or taken a false step and twisted his ankle. He would be lying in the snow, stiff with cold, miserable, lost, perhaps calling out for help, shouting with all the strength of his voice in the silence of the night.

Where could he be? The mountain was so huge, so steep, so dangerous, especially at this time of the year, that it would take ten or twenty guides, searching for a week in all directions, to find a man in that enormous space.

Even so, Ulrich Kunsi made up his mind to take Sam and set out to look for Gaspard, if he had not come back by one o'clock in the morning.

And he made his preparations. He put food for two days into a bag, wound round his waist a long, thin, strong rope, and inspected his stick and the little axe he used for cutting steps in the ice. Then he waited. The fire was blazing in the fireplace, and the big dog lay sleeping before it, lit up by its blaze. The steady ticking of the clock in its wooden case sounded like the beating of a heart.

Still he waited, his ears trying to catch any distant sound. When the breeze lightly touched the roof and the walls, he shivered.

The clock struck midnight. Feeling cold and nervous, he put some water on the fire to boil, so that he might have some really hot coffee before setting out.

Ulrich sets off again

When the clock struck one he got up, woke Sam, opened the door, and set off in the direction of the Wildstrubel. He climbed for five hours, cutting steps in the ice with his axe, always moving steadily forward, and sometimes pulling the dog after him up some steep slope. It was just six o'clock when he reached one of the mountain slopes to which Gaspard often came in search of deer. And there he waited for the dawn.

The sky above him gradually became paler. Then, suddenly, a strange light covered the mountain, stretching for a hundred miles around him. It seemed as though this brightness was rising from the snow to lose itself in space. Gradually the highest mountains in the distance were coloured with a delicate shade of pink, like human flesh, and the red sun appeared from behind the Alps.

Ulrich Kunsi set off again. Like a hunter, he bent down, searching for tracks and saying to his dog, 'Find him, boy! Find him!'

He was now on his way down the mountain, searching everywhere, and sometimes giving a long, loud call, which was quickly lost in the silent spaces. At times he would put his ear close to the ground to listen. He would imagine he heard a voice and he would start running again, shouting as he went. But he heard nothing more, and he would sit down, tired out and in despair. About midday he ate some food and fed Sam, who was as tired as he was. Then once again he set out on his search.

When evening came he was still walking, having covered nearly fifty miles among the mountains. He was too far from the house to think of returning there, and too tired to drag himself along any further. Digging a hole in the snow, he curled up in it with his dog, under a blanket he had brought with him. Man and beast lay together, each body sharing the warmth of the other, but frozen to the bone none the less. Ulrich hardly slept. His mind was full of strange ideas and his limbs were shaking with cold.

When he got up, day was about to dawn. His legs felt as stiff as bars of iron. His spirits were so low that he almost called out in despair, and his heart beat so violently that he nearly fell down with nervousness whenever he imagined that he heard a sound.

The thought suddenly came to him that he too might die of cold in this desert of snow, and the terror at the thought of such a death increased his energy and encouraged him to new effort.

He was now making the descent towards the inn, falling down, picking himself up again, with Sam following far behind, limping along on three legs.

It was four o'clock in the afternoon before they reached the Schwarenbach Inn. There was nobody there. The young man lit a fire, had something to eat, and then fell asleep. He was so tired that he could no longer think.

The voice of a dying man

He slept for a very long time. It seemed as if nothing could disturb him. Then, suddenly, he heard a voice call out 'Ulrich!' It shook him out of his deep sleep and made him sit up. Had he been dreaming? No! He could hear it still. That ringing cry had entered his ear, had entered his body. Beyond all doubt, somebody had shouted, somebody had called out, 'Ulrich!' Then someone must be out there, near the house. There could be no question about it. He opened the door and shouted with all his strength, 'Gaspard, is that you?'

There was no reply. Not a sound, not even a groan*, nothing at all. The snow was dreadfully pale.

The wind had risen. It was that freezing wind which splits the rocks and leaves nothing alive on these lonely heights. Again Ulrich called out, 'Gaspard! Gaspard! Gaspard!'

He waited a little. All was silent on the mountainside. It was then that terror shook him to the very bone. He rushed back into the inn, shut the door, and locked it. Trembling all over, he fell into a chair. He was now absolutely certain that the cry for help had come from his friend, at the very moment when his spirit was leaving his body.

He was as certain of it as people are of being alive or of eating their meals. For two days and three nights, old Gaspard Hari had been lying in some hollow in one of those deep, spotless valleys, whose whiteness is more terrible than darkness in the depths of the earth. For two days and three nights he had been dying, and a moment ago whilst he lay at the point of death, his thoughts had turned to his companion. His soul, as soon as it gained its freedom, had flown to the inn where Ulrich lay sleeping. It had called to him through that mysterious and terrible power by which the souls of the dead haunt* the living. This spirit had called aloud to the soul of the sleeper. It had said its last goodbye, or perhaps its curse, on the man who had given up the search too easily.

And Ulrich felt its presence there, quite near the walls of the house, behind the door which he had just closed. The soul was wandering about like a bird in the night. The desperate young man was ready to scream out in terror. He wanted to run away, but did not dare go out. He did not dare now, nor would he ever dare go outside, for the ghost would be there, day and night, wandering round the inn, until the body

******groan*, a sound made by somebody in pain.
******haunt*, to visit.

of the old guide had been found and laid to rest in the holy ground of a graveyard.

When the morning came Kunsi felt a little better in the brightness of the returning sun. He prepared his breakfast and gave the dog his food. But after that he remained sitting in a chair without moving, his thoughts on the old man who was lying out there in the snow.

The terrors of the night

When night again descended upon the mountains, new terrors attacked him. He walked up and down the kitchen in the dim light of a candle. As he walked he was listening for that cry, which had filled him with terror the night before. Might it not come again, breaking through the silence of the world outside? He felt alone as no man had ever been before, alone in this great desert of snow, alone six thousand feet above the inhabited world, above the homes of men, above busy, noisy, active life. He was alone up here in the frozen sky. He felt a crazy desire to get away, in any direction, by any means. But he did not dare to even open the door. He was sure that the man outside, the dead man, would block his way and prevent him from leaving him all alone in the mountains.

Towards midnight, weary with walking up and down, sick with fright, he finally fell asleep, sitting on a chair. He feared his bed just as he would have feared a place that was haunted.

Suddenly his ears were filled with the same sharp cry that he had heard the night before. It was so loud that Ulrich stretched out his hands to push away the ghost and, losing his balance, he fell backwards on to the floor, taking the chair with him.

Wakened by the noise, Sam began to howl in terror, and ran up and down the room, trying to find out where the danger came from. When he came to the door he smelled at the bottom of it, and began growling, his hair standing on end, his tail stiff.

Beside himself with terror, Kunsi had got up, and seizing his chair by one leg, he shouted, 'Don't come in! Don't come in, or I'll kill you!'

And the dog, excited by this threatening voice, barked furiously at the unseen enemy whom his master was challenging.

Gradually Sam calmed down, and went back to lie by the fire, but he was still uneasy. His eyes were shining and he was baring his teeth and growling.

Ulrich drinks to forget his fear

Ulrich, feeling faint with terror, went to get a bottle of brandy* from the cupboard and drank several glasses of it, one after the other.

On the following day he ate hardly anything but kept on drinking the brandy. For some days after that he was half drunk. As soon as he thought of Gaspard Hari, he would begin drinking, and would not leave off until he fell to the ground. He would lie there face downwards, quite helpless. As soon as he recovered from the efforts of the maddening, burning liquid, the cry 'Ulrich!' would wake him, like a bullet entering his brain. He would get to his feet, walk unsteadily, stretching out his hands to keep himself from falling, and calling to Sam to help him. And the dog, which now seemed to share his master's madness, would throw itself against the door, scratching at it with his claws, biting at it with his long white teeth. Meanwhile, the young man, with his head thrown back, swallowed great mouthfuls of brandy as though he were drinking cold water after a climb in the mountains. Soon his thoughts, his memory, his terror, would be drowned in forgetfulness.

In three weeks he finished all his brandy. But the only effect was to put his terror to sleep. When the drink was no longer there, his fears returned with new power.

He walked up and down his room, now and then putting his ear to the door, listening to see if the other man was there.

And when, completely weary, he fell asleep, he would hear the voice and jump once more to his feet.

At last, one night, with the courage of a coward in despair, he rushed to the door and opened it, to see who was calling him, and to force him to keep quiet.

**brandy*, a strong drink.

The thing outside

The cold air struck him full in the face, and froze him to the bone. He banged the door shut and bolted it, not noticing that Sam had run outside. Shivering, he threw some more wood on the fire and sat down to warm himself. Suddenly he gave a jump. There was someone scratching at the wall and groaning.

He cried out in a voice filled with terror, 'Go away!' He was answered by a long, sad groan.

'Go away!' he cried again, and he turned round and round in an effort to find some corner in which he could hide himself. But the thing outside, continually howling, passed along the front of the house, rubbing itself against the wall. Ulrich rushed to the cupboard, which was full of food and pots, and dragged it across the room and pushed it against the door. Then he took all the remaining furniture and blocked the window, as if he were in a state of war.

But the thing outside went on groaning, and Ulrich himself began to reply with the same kind of strange sound.

Days and nights passed like this, with these two constantly howling at each other. One of them was for ever moving round the house, clawing at the walls, desperately trying to break a way through. The other, inside the inn, sat with his ear close to the wall, following every movement of the thing outside, and answering all its howls with screams of horror.

One evening Ulrich heard nothing more from outside. He dropped into a chair, and he was so worn out that he fell asleep immediately.

When he awoke his mind and memory were a blank. It was as if that sleep had swept everything from his mind. He felt hungry, and took some food.

The Hausers return

The winter was over. The mountain road was open again, and the Hauser family set out on its journey up to the inn.

At the top of the first long climb the two women got on their donkey and talked about the two men whom they would soon meet again.

They were surprised that neither of them had come down a few days earlier, as soon as the road was free, to give them the news of their long winter stay.

They came in sight of the inn, which was still covered with a thick blanket of snow. They saw that the door and window were closed, but old Hauser felt relieved when he saw that smoke was rising from the chimney. As he drew nearer, however, he saw on the door-step the bones of an animal. It was lying on its side, and the flesh had been torn off the bones by the eagles.

They all looked at it.

'It must be Sam,' said Mrs Hauser.

And she called out, 'Hello, Gaspard!' From inside the inn came a cry, like that of an animal. Old Hauser now shouted, 'Hello Gaspard!' A cry just like the first came from inside.

Then the father and his two sons tried to open the door, but it resisted their efforts. From the empty shed they took a wooden beam, and banged it with all their strength against the door, which gave way with a loud crash. They saw that behind the cupboard that had just fallen over, there stood a man. His hair came down to his shoulders, a beard grew down to his chest, his eyes were gleaming brightly, and his clothes were in rags.

They did not recognize him. Then Louise Hauser called out, 'Mother! It's Ulrich!'

And the mother agreed that it was indeed Ulrich, although his hair had turned white.

He let them come up to him, and let them touch him. But when they asked him questions, he made no reply. He had to be taken down to the village where the doctors declared that he was completely mad.

And nobody ever found out what had happened to his companion.

That summer young Louise Hauser was dangerously ill with some mysterious disease. They said it was caused by the cold air of the mountains.

5 The Necklace

She was one of those pretty and charming girls who seem to have been born through some mistake of fortune into the wrong family. She had no money, and no hope of becoming the wife of a rich and famous man. She let herself get married to a badly-paid clerk who worked at the Department of Education in Paris.

She was always unhappy because she felt she had a right to enjoy all kinds of luxuries. She was unhappy because of the poor flat in which she lived, with its shabby walls and shabby furniture. All day long she would think of the beautiful houses of wealthy people.

Each evening, when she sat down at the little round table opposite her husband to eat a very simple meal, she would dream of wonderful dinners served on gleaming silver plates in a magnificent dining-room.

She had no nice dresses, no jewels, nothing expensive. And this was what she wanted most of all. She had a rich school-friend, but she did not like to go and visit her any more because she felt even more unhappy when she got back home.

The invitation

Now, one evening her husband came back from the office and proudly gave her a big envelope.

'Here you are!' he said. 'Here is something that will please you.'

She quickly tore open the envelope and took out a printed card which read:

The Minister of Education and Mrs Ramponneau
are pleased to invite
Mr and Mrs Loisel
to their party on Monday the 18th January.

Instead of being delighted, as her husband had hoped, she threw the invitation angrily onto the table, and said, 'What use is this to me?'

'But, my dear! I thought you'd be pleased. You never go out anywhere, and this is a wonderful opportunity. I had very great difficulty in getting this invitation. Everybody wants to go to the party. Clerks like me are not often invited. You'll see all sorts of important people there.'

She gave him an angry look and then shouted, 'What do you expect me to wear if I go to a party of that kind?'

He had not thought of this.

'Well, what about the dress you wear when you go to the theatre? You look very attractive in that dress.'

He stopped talking. He saw that his wife was crying. Two big tears were slowly running down her cheeks.

'What's the matter? What's the matter?' he asked.

She wiped her damp cheeks and said in a calm voice, 'Nothing. It's just that I haven't a nice dress, so I can't go to the party. Give the invitation to one of your friends, somebody whose wife has better clothes than I have.'

He was very upset and said, 'Look, Matilda. How much would a nice dress cost? I mean one you could use on other occasions, something very simple.'

She thought for a few moments, hesitated, then replied, 'I don't really know, but I think I could get one for 400 francs.'

His face went rather pale. This was exactly the amount of money he had saved to buy a gun so he could go hunting with his friends next summer. But he said, 'All right. I'll give you 400 francs. But try to get a really nice dress.'

Mrs Loisel borrows from her friend

The day of the party was getting near, but Mrs Loisel seemed sad, worried, nervous. Her dress was now ready however.

'What's the matter with you?' asked her husband one evening. 'You've been acting quite strangely for the past three days.'

'I'm annoyed because I haven't any jewellery, nothing to wear with my dress. I shall look really shabby. I almost think I'd rather not go to the party.'

'You can wear some flowers.' he replied. 'They are very fashionable at this time of the year. For ten francs you can get two or three magnificent roses.'

But he could not persuade her.

'No,' she answered. 'There's nothing worse than looking shabby amongst a lot of wealthy women.'

'How silly you are!' cried her husband. 'Go and see your friend Mrs Forester and ask her to lend you some jewellery. You know her well enough to be able to make such a request.'

'That's true,' she said cheerfully. 'I'd not thought of that!'

The next day she went to see her friend and told her what her problem was.

Mrs Forester went over to a cupboard and took out a large box of jewellery.

'Choose anything you like, my dear,' she said.

Mrs Loisel saw that the box contained bracelets, a pearl necklace, a cross, and all kinds of jewellery in gold and precious stones. She tried some of it on in front of the mirror, hesitating, not being able to decide which she wanted to wear. She kept asking, 'Haven't you anything else?'

'Of course. See what you can find. There should be something there that will please you.'

Suddenly she discovered a magnificent diamond necklace in a box lined with black silk. Her heart began to beat faster. Her fingers trembled as she lifted it out of the box. She fastened it round her throat against the high-necked dress and looked at herself in the mirror with absolute delight.

Then she asked, hesitating and nervous in case Mrs Forester should refuse, 'Would you lend me this, just this?'

'Yes, of course!'

She threw her arms round her friend's neck and kissed her in her excitement. Then she went home as fast as she could with her treasure.

The evening of the party

The day of the party arrived. Mrs Loisel was a great success. She looked prettier than all the other women. She was charming, graceful, all smiles, beside herself with joy. All the men were staring at her, asking who she was, trying to get introduced. Everybody wanted to dance with her. Even the Minister of Education noticed her.

She danced wildly, with great pleasure, thinking of nothing but the triumph of her beauty, the glory of her success. She danced in a kind of cloud of happiness formed by all this praise, all this admiration, all this feeling of victory so dear to a woman's heart.

She did not leave the party until four o'clock in the morning. Since midnight her husband had been in a little room, fast asleep, with three other gentleman whose wives were enjoying themselves.

She put on her ordinary, everyday coat, and its shabbiness showed up against her elegant party dress. As soon as she saw this she wanted to get away as quickly as possible so she would not be noticed by the other women who were dressing themselves in rich furs.

'Wait a minute,' said her husband. 'You'll catch a cold out in the street. I'm going to get a taxi.'

But she was not listening to him, and was hurrying down the stairs. When they got into the street they could not find a taxi. They looked everywhere, shouting across to the taxi-drivers they saw in the distance.

They walked down to the River Seine, desperate, shivering with the cold. At last they found near the river-bank one of those shabby old taxis which you only see in Paris after dark – as though they are too ashamed to appear in the streets in daylight.

It took them back home and they sadly climbed the stairs to their flat. For Mrs Loisel it was all over. And her husband was thinking that he would have to be in his office at the Ministry of Education by ten o'clock.

The necklace has gone

She took off her coat and stood in front of the mirror so she could see herself once more in all her glory.

Suddenly she gave a cry. The diamond necklace was no longer there.

Her husband, already half undressed, asked her, 'What's the matter with you?'

She turned towards him, frightened and upset, 'I've. . . I've . . . lost Mrs Forester's necklace!'

He stood up in alarm.

'What? How can you have lost it? It's not possible!'

They searched in the folds of her dress, in the coat, in the pockets, everywhere. But they could not find it.

'Are you sure you were still wearing it when you left the party?' he asked.

'Yes. I remember touching it just before we left.'

'If you lost it in the street we would have heard it drop. It must be in the taxi.'

'Yes. It probably is. Did you take the number of the taxi?'

'No. Did you notice what it was?'

'No.'

They stared at each other, not knowing what to do. Then Loisel got dressed again.

'I'll go over the whole distance we came on foot, just in case it's in the street.'

He went out, and she remained sitting in a chair, still in her party dress, without the strength to go to bed, or to light a fire, or even to think.

Her husband came back at about seven o'clock in the morning. He had not found anything.

They went to the police station and to the newspaper offices, where they advertised for it, offering a reward. They went round to the taxi companies, anywhere, in fact, where there was any hope of finding the necklace.

She spent the whole of that day in a state of terror, thinking of the terrible event which had happened to them.

Loisel came home that evening, his face pale, his cheeks hollow. He had not been able to discover anything.

'You'll have to write to your friend,' he said, 'and tell her that you have broken the necklace and that you are having it repaired. That should give us time to go on searching.'

She wrote the letter exactly as he told her.

The Loisels buy another necklace

By the end of another week they had lost all hope.

Loisel, who now looked five years older, said to his wife, 'We shall have to think about buying another necklace to replace the one we've lost.'

The next day they took the empty box which had contained it and went to the jeweller whose name was written inside. He looked at his books.

'I was not the person who sold this necklace, madam,' he said. 'I must have supplied only the box.'

Then they went round from jeweller to jeweller, searching for a necklace exactly like the one they had lost, both of them ill with sorrow and anxiety.

In a shop in the Palais Royal they found a diamond necklace which looked exactly like the one they were searching for. The price was 40,000 francs, but the jeweller said they could have it for 36,000.

He promised them he would not sell it for another three days and said he would buy it back from them for 34,000 francs if the first necklace was found by the end of February.

Loisel had 18,000 francs which his father had left him. He would have to borrow the rest.

So he started to borrow, asking for a thousand francs from one person, five hundred from another, dealing with money-lenders, signing his name without knowing whether he would ever be able to pay back the money. Filled with horror as he thought of the future and the awful misery of the life they would now lead, he went to the jeweller's and bought the diamond necklace, paying him 36,000 francs.

When Mrs Loisel took the necklace back, Mrs Forester said, looking rather annoyed, 'You should have brought it back sooner than this. I might have wanted to wear it.'

She did not open the box, which was what Mrs Loisel was afraid she might do. If she had noticed that it was not the same necklace what would she have thought of her? Would she not have thought her a thief?

A life of poverty

Mrs Loisel now had to live the dreadful life of those who are really poor. But she made up her mind to be brave about it. This terrible debt had to be paid, and she would pay it! She dismissed the girl who had been their servant, and they left their home, renting a small room right at the top of a big, old house.

Now she had to do all the housework herself and all the dirty jobs in the kitchen. She washed the pots and wore out her pink fingernails as she scraped clean the bottoms of pans. She washed the dirty sheets, shirts and towels, and hung them out on a line to dry. Every morning she took the rubbish down into the street and carried up the buckets of water, stopping on each floor in order to get her breath back. Dressed like an ordinary poor woman she went out shopping, carrying her basket, arguing about prices, hearing the shopkeepers swear at her as she defended her miserable bit of money.

Her husband did extra work in the evening copying figures for businessmen at a few pence a page.

This life went on for ten years. At the end of this time they had paid all the money back, every penny of it, including all the interest.

Mrs Loisel looked old now. She had become the strong, tough, coarse kind of woman often seen in poor districts. Her hair was never properly combed, her dress always looked untidy, and she talked in a loud voice as she scrubbed the floors. But sometimes, when her husband was at the office she could sit by the window and dream of that night long ago, of that party where she had been so beautiful and so much admired.

To think what might have happened if she had not lost that necklace! Who could tell? How strange life is! How quickly it changes! How little it takes to bring you happiness or misery!

A terrible discovery

Now, one Sunday, as she was walking in the centre of Paris

to get some fresh air after all the hard work of the week, she suddenly noticed a woman who was taking a child for a walk. It was Mrs Forester, still young, still beautiful, still attractive.

Mrs Loisel felt very nervous. Should she go and speak to her? Yes, of course. Now she had paid all her debts, she would tell her the whole story. Why not?

She went up to her and said, 'Hello, Jean!'

Her friend did not recognize her and was, in fact, very surprised that this shabby woman should speak to her in such a familiar way.

'Madam,' she said, 'I don't think I know you. You must have mistaken me for someone else.'

'No! I'm Matilda Loisel!'

Her friend gave a cry of amazement.

'Oh! My poor Matilda! How you have changed!'

'Ah, yes. I've passed through some very hard times since I saw you last, and I've had a lot of unhappiness, and all because of you!'

'Because of me? What do you mean?'

'Do you remember that diamond necklace you lent me when I went to the party at the Ministry?'

'Yes, I do. What about it?'

'Well, I lost it.'

'What? How can you have lost it? You brought it back to me.'

'I brought back another necklace exactly like it. And we've been paying for it for the last ten years. You can imagine how hard it has been for us, because we had so little money. Ah, well! It's all over now, and I'm thankful that it is.'

'Are you telling me that you bought a diamond necklace to replace the one I lent you?'

'Yes. You didn't notice the difference, did you? They were exactly alike!'

And she was so proud and pleased that she gave a smile.

Mrs Forester, terribly upset, took both her friend's hands in her own.

'Oh! My poor Matilda! My diamond necklace was imitation! It was worth 500 francs at the most!'

6 A Vendetta

Paul Saverini's widow lived with her son in a little house in Bonifacio on the island of Corsica. The town is built on the slope of a mountain and, in places, it even hangs over the sea.

On the white mountain-side, the houses look like birds' nests fastened to the rock, and they look down on this terrible sea through which ships rarely find it safe to go. The wind constantly whips up the waves, constantly wears away the bare coast and rushes through the narrow sea between Corsica and Sardinia, attacking the land on each side.

Mother Saverini's house was built into the very edge of the cliff. It had three windows, each of which looked out onto this wild and lonely scene.

There she lived, all alone, except for her son, Antony, and their dog, Sémillante. It was a large thin creature with a rough coat and looked like a sheep-dog. The young man always used to take her as his gun-dog when he went hunting.

One evening there was a quarrel, and Antony Saverini was murdered by Nicolas Ravolati, who killed him with a knife and managed to get across to Sardinia the same night.

When they brought the body back to the old widow she did not cry, but stood there for a long time, absolutely still. Then she stretched out her old hand over the body and promised her son a vendetta. She did not want anyone to stay with her, and she shut herself in with the body, accompanied only by the dog, which was howling. This animal went on howling, standing at the foot of the bed. Its head was turned to one side and it was looking at its master, with its tail between its legs. It made no more movement than the mother, who was now bending over the body, staring hard, and shedding great silent tears.

The young man was lying on his back and wearing his rough jacket which was torn and cut about the chest. He looked as though he was asleep. But there was blood all over him – on his shirt, which had been torn when they had tried to give first aid, and on his waistcoat, his trousers, his hands, his face. Blood had also dried in his beard and his hair.

The mother promises revenge

The old mother began to talk to him. At the sound of her voice the dog stopped howling.

'There, there! You'll be revenged my dear son, my poor child. Go to sleep now, go to sleep. You'll be revenged. Do you hear me? It's your mother who promises your revenge! And she always keeps her promise, you know that, don't you?'

And slowly she bent closer to him and pressed her cold lips against the dead lips of her son.

Then Sémillante started to howl again, a long, sad sound, terrible to hear.

They both remained there, the woman and the dog, until dawn.

Antony Saverini was buried that day, and soon the people of Bonifacio were no longer talking about him.

He had left behind neither brother nor any near cousins. There was no man who could carry out the vendetta. But all alone his old mother was thinking about it.

From morning till night she stared at a white point on the coast on the other side. It was the little Sardinian village of Longosardo, where Corsican criminals go to hide when they are being hunted. They form almost the entire population of this little village which looks across to the coast of their home-land. There they wait until it is safe to come back and start their ordinary life again. She knew very well that Nicolas Ravolati was hiding in this village.

All alone, all day long, she sat by her window looking across at the village, thinking of revenge. How would she be able to manage it, with no one to help her and with so little strength and such a short time to live? But she had made a promise. She had sworn over the body of her son. She could not forget, and she could not wait. How could she manage it? She never slept at night now, she could find no rest. She was searching for a solution, refusing to give up. At her feet the dog lay asleep, but sometimes she would raise her head and howl into the distance. Ever since her master's death she often howled like this as if she were calling to him.

Now, one night, just as Sémillante was starting to howl again, the old mother suddenly had an idea. She thought about it all night long and then, as soon as it was light, she got up and went to the church. She prayed, lying on the stone floor, asking God to help her. She asked him to give to her poor tired body the strength she would need to take revenge for her son.

The old woman starts to train the dog

Then she went back home. She had in her yard an old barrel which collected the water which came down from the roof. She turned it over on its side to empty it, then fixed it firmly to the ground, holding it in position by means of stones and wooden posts. Then she chained Sémillante to this kennel*, and finally went back into the house.

Now she began to walk up and down her room, never taking her eyes off the Sardinian coast. There was the murderer, just over there!

The dog howled all day long and all through the night. In the morning the old woman brought her some water in a bowl, but nothing else: no soup, no bread, nothing.

Another day went by. Sémillante, weak and tired by now, spent the time asleep. The next morning the dog's eyes were gleaming, her hair was standing on end, and she was pulling wildly on her chain.

Once again the old woman gave her nothing to eat. The animal was now almost crazy and it was barking with a strange voice. Another night went by.

Then, as soon as it was light, Mother Saverini went round to her neighbour's house to ask if she might have two bundles of straw. She took some old clothes which her husband had

******kennel,* small shelter for a dog.

once worn, and stuffed them with the straw until they looked like the body of a man.

She then stuck a strong post into the ground in front of Sémillante's kennel and tied this dummy* to it so that it looked as though it was standing up. Then she made a head for it out of a bundle of old underclothes.

The dog, surprised and puzzled, stared at this man of straw, and stopped barking, even though she was desperately hungry.

Now the old woman went to the butcher's shop and bought some sausage. When she got back home she took some sticks and lit a fire in her yard near the kennel, and then roasted her sausage on it. Sémillante, crazy with hungry, started jumping about, and all the time her eyes were on the roasting sausage, whose delicious smell was entering her stomach.

Then the old mother took this steaming food and with it made a neck-tie for the straw dummy. She spent a long time fastening it round the neck, threading it so that it actually went inside. When she had finished she let the dog off the chain.

In one great leap the animal reached the dummy's throat and began to tear it out, with its paws resting on the shoulders. It got down with a piece of the food in its mouth, then leaped up again. It buried its teeth in the neck and tore out a few more pieces of food. It kept jumping up and down working away as though it had gone mad. With savage bites it tore away the face and reduced the whole of the neck to rags.

Standing there still and silent, the old woman looked on with a strange gleam in her eyes. Then she chained the animal up again, gave it no food for another two days, then started this strange performance all over again. For three months she accustomed it to this desperate struggle. Now she no longer needed to keep it on a chain. At the slightest sign from its mistress it would leap upon the dummy.

She had taught the dog to tear the throat savagely to pieces, even when there was no food hidden there. But as a reward she always gave it the sausage which she had just roasted.

**dummy*, a figure of a man.

As soon as Sémillante caught sight of the man of straw she would tremble with excitement, then look at her mistress waiting for her to raise her finger and shout in her squeaking voice, 'Now!'

The old woman visits her son's murderer

When she thought that the time had come, Mother Saverini found some man's clothes and disguished herself as an old shabby beggar. Next she paid a Sardinian fisherman to take her across to the other side.

In a cloth bag she carried a large piece of sausage. Sémillante had been kept without food for two whole days. Every now and then the old woman let her smell the food, in order to excite her.

Soon they reached the village of Longosardo. The old Corsican widow went limping along until she came to a baker's shop where she asked if they could tell her where Nicolas Ravolati lived. He had gone back to his previous job as a carpenter, and he was working at the back of his workshop.

The old woman pushed open the door and called out, 'Hello, there, Nicolas!'

He turned round. Letting the dog go, she shouted, 'Now! Now! Food! Food!'

The half-crazy animal went for his throat. The man stretched out his arms then fell, rolling on the floor, struggling with the dog. For a few seconds he lay there, kicking out with his feet. Then he became absolutely still as Sémillante bit into his throat, tearing it to pieces.

Two neighbours, who had been sitting in their doorways, clearly remembered having seen an old beggar leave the house. With him was a thin black dog which was eating something brown, and being fed by its master as they went along.

By evening the old woman had got back home again. That night she slept well.

7 The Unknown

The train was travelling at full speed through the darkness. I was the only person there except for an old gentleman who was sitting opposite me, looking out of the window.

There was no moon, and the night was so hot we could hardly breathe. You could not even see any stars and as the train rushed on, the air coming through the window felt like some hot, soft material, heavy and choking. We had left Paris three hours earlier and we were now somewhere near the centre of France, though we could see nothing at all of the countryside through which we were travelling.

Suddenly, we saw something which seemed just like magic – two men standing round a big fire in the middle of the forest.

We only saw the scene for a second or two, but we had a clear view of two miserable-looking beggars, dressed in rags and gleaming red from the glow of their great blazing fire. Their bearded faces were turned towards us, and all round them there were the green trees, standing out in the reflected blaze, with their leaves all covered by the spreading fire-light.

Then the scene disappeared and everything was absolutely black again.

What a strange thing to see! What were these two wandering beggars doing in that forest? Why had they lit this big fire on such a hot night?

The old gentleman sitting opposite me pulled out his watch and remarked, 'It's exactly midnight, sir. What an amazing sight we've just seen.'

I agreed with him, and we began to talk, discussing who these two strange men might be. Were they criminals burning the evidence, or were they performing magic? After all, you don't light a fire like that in the middle of the night at the height of summer, just to make soup. So what were they doing? We simply couldn't think of any likely explanation.

The old man's strange conversation

My travelling companion now settled down to talk. He was a fairly old man. I never managed to discover his profession. He was very well-educated and definitely peculiar. I even had the feeling that he might have been a little mad.

'I'm glad I saw that,' he said. 'During those few moments I experienced a feeling which men hardly know now. How disturbing the world must have been in those far-off days when life was full of mystery!

'As we find explanations for things we didn't previously understand, we gradually empty the world of the imagination. Don't you agree with me, sir, that the night has become really empty? It is little more than a sort of ordinary black thing, now that men no longer believe it contains ghosts. People are saying, "No more magic, no more strange beliefs!" All the things which were once mysterious have now been explained. With each new day science pushes back the frontiers of what was once amazing and mysterious.

'Well, sir, I belong to the group of older people who still want to believe, who are quite accustomed not to understand or know for certain. We have grown up surrounded by mystery and we refuse to accept simple truth. Nowadays, the earth seems to me like an abandoned world, empty and bare. All beliefs which gave poetry to life have now disappeared.

'When I go out in the dark, how I should love to tremble with that feeling of terror which causes old women to make the sign of the cross when they pass the walls of a graveyard. How I wish I could believe in some dim horror which people used to imagine they could sense hiding in the darkness!

'How frightening the dark shadows of evening must have been in the old days, when the darkness was full of strange beings! Although people had no idea of what these ghosts and devils looked like, their presence was so real that it froze the heart with horror. Their hidden power so great that it seemed impossible to escape from them.

'If we suddenly found ourselves alone in that forest we should never be able to forget the sight of those two strange men in the glow of their fire. And we should fear them far more than any kind of actual danger. Yes, we are truly afraid only of things we do not understand.'

Turgenev's story

At that moment there came into my mind a story which Turgenev had told us one Sunday at Gustave Flaubert's place. I've no idea whether or not he has ever included it in any of his books.

This great Russian writer has no equal when it comes to being able to excite and frighten the reader with the mysterious unknown. In his stories you can really feel that fear of the Unseen, the fear of something strange behind a wall, behind a door, something hidden beneath the world we can see. He tells us simple stories in which there is just the hint of something mysterious and disturbing. On that particular day he, too, happened to remark: 'We are truly afraid only of the things we do not understand.'

There he was in that big armchair, with his arms hanging over the sides, his legs stretched out before him, and with his face almost lost in that great white beard and long silver hair.

He spoke slowly and seemed to relive every moment of his strange experience, and his pale eyes would occasionally open wide and light up with excitement, just as a child's eyes do when they are telling a story.

This was what he told us on that occasion:

In his younger days he used to go hunting in the forests of Russia. One day he had done a lot of hard walking, and towards the end of the afternoon he came to the banks of a peaceful river.

It was flowing along full of floating weeds, and the water was deep, cold and clear.

The hunter felt a strong urge to jump into this perfectly clear water. He got undressed, and dived in. He was a very tall and strong young man, and a powerful swimmer.

He allowed himself to float gently along, enjoying the feeling of peaceful rest as the water-weeds and roots and hanging leaves brushed lightly against his flesh.

A monster's hand on his shoulder

Suddenly, he felt a hand on his shoulder. What a shock!

He immediately turned round, and saw a terrible creature staring at him with greedy eyes.

It seemed to be half-woman and half-monkey. The creature had a huge twisted face, and long hair, which hung round her face and floated on the water above her back.

Turgenev felt himself freezing with horror.

Without a moment's thought he started to swim wildly for the river-bank. But the monster swam even faster, and it kept touching his neck, his back and his legs, giving little laughs of delight.

The young man, absolutely terrified, finally reached the bank, and ran off as fast as he could through the wood. He did not even think about trying to find his clothes and his gun.

The dreadful creature came after him, running just as fast as he did, and growling at him all the time.

Absolutely exhausted, he was on the point of dropping to the ground when a child appeared. The child, who was looking after some goats, was holding a whip, and with it he began to hit the terrible human monster, which ran away howling with pain. And Turgenev saw it disappearing into the trees, looking like a great female monkey.

It was, in fact, a crazy old woman, who had lived in this wood for more than thirty years, living on food provided by the kindness of the farmers who owned the goats. She spent half her time swimming in the river.

The great Russian author added this remark, 'I've never been so frightened in the whole of my life. And it was all because I just couldn't understand what this monster could be.'

The old man's frightening experience

Well, I told this story to my travelling companion, and when I had finished, he said once more, 'Ah, yes. We're only afraid of the things we don't understand. I once had a personal experience of the full force of terror, and it was caused by such a simple, silly thing, that I am almost too ashamed to tell you about it.

'At that time I was on a walking tour through Brittany, all by myself. I had just finished walking across Finistère, a place that is almost a desert, where nothing grows except tiny bushes, from the midst of which rise great sacred stones from ancient times. The place made me think of ghosts, and my mind was full of the stories that are written or told about this region of strange beliefs.

'It was night-time, and I was walking along a flat coastline. It was so low, in fact, that it seemed to be below sea-level. Wherever I looked I could see the grey threatening sea, with sharp rocks sticking out.

'I had eaten my dinner in a fisherman's inn and was now walking along the road, which ran in a perfectly straight line along the coast. It was very dark.

'Every now and then a tall stone set up by an ancient tribe suddenly appeared out of the darkness. It looked like a ghost which was standing absolutely still and staring at me as I passed. Gradually, I felt myself becoming nervous. I couldn't really say why. There are evenings when you have the feeling of being lightly touched by the dead, when you tremble for no particular reason. Your heart beats faster because you experience the terror of the unseen – that mysterious unseen which I personally wish were still part of life.

'How long this road seemed! It seemed to go on for ever, and I felt so very lonely.

'There was no sound except the thunder of the distant waves somewhere behind me. Sometimes this steady, dangerous sound seemed so close to me that I imagined the waves were almost touching my heels, rolling over the plain towards me. I felt as though I ought to set off and run as fast as my legs would carry me in order to escape the tide.

'The wind was not very strong, but it was blowing and whistling through the bushes all round me. And though I was walking quite fast, my legs and arms were cold, with that unpleasant cold feeling which you experience when you are afraid.

'Oh, how I longed to meet another human! It was now so dark that I could hardly see the road.

'Suddenly, I heard a low rattling noise coming from some distance ahead of me. I thought, "Hello! That sounds like a cart." Then I heard nothing more.

'A minute later I heard the same noise again, only this time it was getting nearer.

'I could see no light of any kind, but I said to myself, "I suppose they've no lamp on the cart. There's nothing surprising about that in this wild district."

'The noise stopped once more, then started again. It didn't seem to come from anything as heavy as a cart. Besides, I couldn't hear the sound of a horse pulling it, which rather surprised me, because the night was quiet enough for me to have heard this.

'I began to ask myself, "What on earth can it be?"

'It was now coming rapidly towards me, very rapidly! I was certain now that the noise was being made by a single wheel. There were no running footsteps of any kind. What on earth was it?

The cart was moving by itself

It was now very close, almost upon me. With a movement of fear I jumped out of the way into a ditch, and I saw passing right in front of me a little cart with a single wheel, running along all by itself, with nobody pushing it. Yes, a little cart, all by itself.

'My heart started to beat so violently that I fell back into the grass and lay there listening to the sound of the wheel, which was gradually fading away as it went towards the sea. And I was too terrified to stand up, or walk, or make any kind of movement, for if it had come back, if it had come after me, I should have died of terror.

'It was a very long time before I recovered. And I completed my journey along the road in such a state of nervousness that the slightest unexpected sound took my breath away.

'It was silly of me I know. But I was absolutely terrified.

'When I thought it over, some time afterwards, I realised what it must have been. The cart was being pushed along by some child who had bare feet. But I had expected to see a man pushing it, and had looked for his head at the normal height.

'Just try to imagine how I felt. My mind was already being influenced by the strange scenery and stories of ghosts. Then there was this little cart, running along all by itself. I was absolutely terrified!'

8 A Nightmare in Paris

I am extremely fond of the night. I love it in the way that men love their country, with a love that is deep and lasts for ever. I love it with every one of my senses – with my eyes which see it, with my sense of smell which breathes it in, with my ears which listen to its silence, with the whole of my body which feels the gentle touch of its darkness.

I am tired and bored by the daylight. It is rough and noisy. I hate to get up, to get dressed, to go out. Every movement, every word, every thought tires me as though I was lifting some great heavy weight.

But when the sun goes down, a strange delight fills my whole body. I wake up. I come alive. As the darkness increases I feel a different sort of person – younger, stronger, livelier, happier.

Then I feel like shouting with delight and running along the roof-tops, like the cats. I walk on and on, sometimes through the streets of Paris, sometimes through the neighbouring woods, where I can hear the footsteps of creatures like myself which come out only at night.

The thing that you love violently always kills you in the end. But how can I explain what it is that comes over me? How can I even make myself understood so that I can tell the story? I don't know. I simply don't know. All I know is that it's there.

Well, anyhow, yesterday – or was it yesterday? Yes, surely it was – unless it happened earlier, some other day, some other month, some other year. I don't really know. Yet it must have been yesterday because there's been no dawn since it happened, there's been no sunrise. But how long has this night lasted? Who can tell? Who will ever know?

Well, yesterday, then , I went out after dinner, as I do every evening. It was fine, very mild and warm. As I walked down towards the main streets I looked up at the black sky full of stars.

Everything shone brightly in the clear air, everything from the stars above me to the gas lamps on earth. So many lights were burning up there and in the city that the very darkness seemed to be alive. Bright nights like this are much more delightful than days of bright sunshine.

Along the streets the cafés* were blazing with light. People were laughing, moving about, sitting and drinking. I went into to a theatre for a short while. Which theatre was it? I can't remember. It was so brightly lit in there that it upset me, and I came out again.

I walked along a street in the centre of Paris where the open-air cafés looked like blazing fireplaces amongst the trees, and the electric lights, like pale moons, made the gas lamps seem ugly and dirty.

I went into the woods and walked there for a long, long time. Then I came back towards the city.

**café*, a place where you can buy drinks, especially coffee.

I don't really know what time it was. The city was now asleep, and great black clouds were slowly spreading across the sky.

A strange feeling

For the first time I felt that I was going to be a witness of something strange, something new. It seemed to be getting cold, and the air seemed somehow thicker. I felt as though the night, my lovely night, was weighing heavily upon my heart.

The famous avenue was lonely now. There were just two policemen, all alone, walking along the taxi rank. A row of carts full of vegetables was on its way to the market. They were moving along slowly piled high with all kinds of vegetables. The drivers were asleep, hidden from view, and the horses were walking along steadily, following the carts in front of them, making no noise on the roadway. As they passed each gas lamp at the edge of the pavement, the carrots showed up red under the light, the turnips white and the cabbages green. And they passed along, one after the other, these carts which were red like fire, white like silver, and green like the sea. I followed them, then I turned into Royal Street and got back onto the main streets. There was nobody about now, no brightly-lit cafés – just one or two people who had stayed out late and were hurrying back home. I had never seen Paris so dead and lonely. I took out my watch. It was two o'clock in the morning.

Some kind of force was urging me on, compelling me to continue walking. So I continued as far as Bastille Square. It was there that I realised that I had never experienced a night as black as this. A thick blanket of cloud had covered the stars and now seemed to be descending to destroy the earth.

Where is everyone?

I walked back the way I had come. The only person I saw was a drunk who nearly walked into me and then he, too, disappeared into the night. For some time I could hear his unsteady steps echoing through the darkness. I walked on. In front of the Vaudeville Theatre a rag-and-bone man was searching in the gutter. His little lantern was swinging about close to the ground. I asked him, 'What time is it, old man?'

He muttered, 'How should I know? I haven't got a watch.'

Then I suddenly realised that all the gas lamps had gone out. I know they turn them off early at this time of the year to save money. But they do it towards dawn, and dawn was still very far away.

'Come on!' I said to myself. 'Let's go to the market. At least there'll be some life down there.'

I set off, but I couldn't even see to find my way. I moved forward very slowly, as you do in the middle of a wood, recognising the streets by counting them as I went.

In front of a bank a dog growled at me. I turned down another street, got lost, then found my way again. The whole of Paris was asleep, lost in a deep and dreadful sleep. But in the distance I heard a cab rattling along. I tried to reach it, in the direction of the sound made by its wheels, feeling my way along lonely streets as dark as death.

I was lost again. Where was I? How silly to put the gas lamps out so early! There was not a single person in the streets, not a single person going home late. Not even a cat. Nothing at all.

Where on earth were the police? I thought, 'I'll call out. Surely a policeman will come and help me.' I called out. Nobody answered.

I called out even louder. My voice was lost in the darkness, weak, without any echo, as though choked into silence by the night.

I yelled out, 'Help! Help! Help!' My cry of despair remained unanswered. What time could it be then? I pulled out my watch, but I had no matches with me so I could not see it. With a strange pleasure I listened to the faint ticking of this tiny piece of machinery. It seemed like something alive. I felt less lonely now. How strange! I set off again, feeling my way like a blind man, tapping along the walls with my walking-stick, and every now and then I would look up at the sky, hoping to see some gleam of dawn. But the heavens were black, even blacker than the city.

What could the time be? I seemed to have been walking for ages. My legs were ready to give way under me, I was short of breath, and aching with a terrible hunger.

Was anyone alive?

I decided that I would ring the first door bell I came to. I pulled the brass handle, and the ringing of the bell echoed through the house. It was a strange kind of ring, as though this trembling sound was the only thing alive in the house.

I waited, but there was no answer, and nobody opened the door. I rang once again, and waited again. Nothing!

I became frightened. I ran to the house next door, and twenty times I rapidly rang the bell in the dark entrance-hall where the servant would be sleeping. But he did not wake up. And I went on and on, down the street, pulling the bells as hard as I could, banging with my hands and feet and my stick on these doors which refused to open.

Then I suddenly realised that I had reached the market. There was nobody there. Not a sound, not a movement, not a cart, not a single person. Not a bundle of vegetables or a bunch of flowers. The place was empty, abandoned, dead!

A feeling of horror came over me. What was happening? Oh, my God! What was happening?

I set off again. But what time was it? What time was it? Who would tell me the time? Not a single clock had struck in any of the churches or public buildings. I thought, 'I know. I'll open the front of my watch and feel the position of the hands with my fingers.' I pulled out my watch. It wasn't ticking any more. It had stopped.

Nothing now, nothing. Not the least movement in the city, not a single gleam of light, not the slightest sound. Nothing! Not even the sound of the distant taxi!

I had reached the River Seine, and I could feel the cold damp rising from the river. Was the Seine still flowing?

I had to know. I found the steps and went down. I couldn't

hear the water rushing under the bridge. A few more steps, then there was sand, then mud, then water. I pushed my arm deep into the water. Yes, it was flowing, cold, almost frozen, almost dried up, almost dead.

And I knew only too well that I should never have the strength to get back up again, that I too was going to die there, of hunger, weakness and cold.

Then I woke up. The nightmare was over.

9 Coco

The farm belonging to the Lucas family was the largest and the best organised in the whole district.

The farm-yard was enormous and surrounded by five rows of magnificent trees which sheltered the little tender apple-trees from the fierce winds which blew from the plain. Round the yard were long buildings which were used to store cattle-food and grain. There were fine cow-sheds built in good hard stone, stables big enough for thirty horses, and a red brick farm-house which looked like a small castle.

Every day at noon fifteen people – masters, farm-lads, and servants – sat down round the long table in the kitchen, before a big bowl decorated with blue flowers which was filled with steaming hot soup.

All the farm animals – horses, cows, pigs and sheep – were well-fed and well looked after. Mr Lucas, a tall man who was developing quite a stomach, used to make his tour of inspection three times a day, to keep an eye on things and see that all was in order.

In a corner of the stables was a very old white horse, which they kept simply out of kindness. The farmer's wife wanted to have him fed and looked after until he died of old age, because she had brought him up herself and had grown very attached to him, and had many happy memories connected with him.

This old retired horse was looked after by a farm-lad called Isidore Duval, known simply as Zidore. In the winter months he would give him his share of corn and hay. In summer he was supposed to go four times a day to the hillside where the horse was tied up and move him round so that he would have plenty of fresh grass to eat.

The animal was very lame and it was with difficulty that he lifted his heavy legs which were swollen at the knees and just above the feet. His coat, which nobody ever brushed nowadays, looked as though it was made of white human hair, and very long eye-lashes gave him a sad expression.

When Zidore took him out to the fields the horse moved so slowly that he had to pull hard on the rope, and the lad, bent double and breathing hard, used to curse and swear at him, annoyed that he had to look after such a miserable old horse.

When the farm-hands realised how annoyed he was with Coco, they began to make fun of him.

The lad became very angry and he began to feel a growing desire to take revenge on the old horse. He was a thin, long-legged boy, always very dirty. People thought he was stupid because he spoke with a good deal of effort, as though ideas were very slow to form in his mind.

For a long time now he had not been able to understand why they kept Coco, and he was very upset to see good food wasted on this useless creature. Since Coco had stopped working it seemed quite wrong to go on feeding him. In spite of the strict orders he had received from Monsieur Lucas he would often save some of the horse's food, giving him only half the corn and hay he needed. And in the dim mind of this lad there grew a hatred for the horse, the hatred of a country-boy who was greedy, cunning and cruel.

Zidore's cruelty begins

When summer came round again he had to go and move the horse so that it could eat the grass on different parts of the hillside. It was quite a distance. Every morning the lad became more and more annoyed as he slowly made his way through the cornfields. The men who were out working used to call out to him in fun, 'Hello, there, Zidore! Give my best wishes to Coco!'

He never replied, but he would break off a long branch as he passed along the hedges, and when he had moved the post to which the old horse was tied, he would wait until he had started feeding again, then he would creep up from behind and whip the back of the animal's legs with the branch. The poor horse would try to run away, try to kick out, try to get away from the blows, and he would move round and round the post, like an animal in a circus-ring. The lad would run round after him, hitting out violently, showing his teeth in anger.

Then he would slowly walk away without looking round, while the horse watched him out of his old eyes, with his thin sides moving in and out as he breathed hard with having been made to gallop. And he would never bend his white head to eat the grass until he had seen the lad's blue jacket disappear from sight.

As the nights were warm now they let old Coco sleep out in the open, near the valley, just beyond the wood. Zidore was the only one who went out to see him.

The boy now amused himself by throwing stones at him. He would sit down on the slope, about ten yards above him, and for as long as half an hour at a time he would keep throwing sharp-edged stones at the poor old horse. Coco stood there, tied to the post in front of his enemy, keeping his eyes on him all the time and never daring to start eating the grass again until he had gone.

The boy decides to starve the horse

One thought filled the farm-lad's mind. Why should he go on feeding this horse which no longer did any work? It seemed to him that this miserable animal was stealing food which belonged to others, stealing what belonged to men and what the Good Lord provided, stealing even from him, Zidore, who had to work for his living.

And so, gradually, day by day, the lad reduced the area on which the horse could feed, moving the wooden post less and less.

The animal was now desperately hungry, growing thin, wasting away. He was too weak to break the rope, so he stretched his head in an effort to reach the tall green grass, gleaming in the sunlight. It was so close that he could smell its sweet scent, and yet it was just out of his reach.

But one morning Zidore had a better idea. He decided he would not move Coco at all. He was really tired of walking all that way just to look after an old bag of bones.

Nevertheless, he went out to see him, so he could enjoy his revenge. The poor creature stared at him anxiously. But on this particular day Zidore did not hit the horse. He simply walked round and round him, hands in pockets. He even pretended he was going to change the position of the post. But he banged it firmly back in exactly the same hole, and then he went off, delighted with his new trick.

When the horse saw him going away he neighed* as though to call him back, but the farm-lad broke into a run, leaving old Coco all alone in the little valley, firmly attached, without a single blade of grass within reach of his jaws.

Crazy with hunger he tried to reach the rich, green grass which he could only touch with the end of his nose. He went down in his knees, stretched his neck, and reached as far as he possibly could with his mouth. But it was no use.

During the whole of that day the old animal tired himself out in useless, desperate efforts. He was tortured* by hunger and his torture was made even more terrible by the sight of delicious green food stretching into the distance.

The farm-lad did not come back at all that day. He was wandering through the woods, looking for birds' nests.

He turned up the following day. Coco, absolutely worn out, was now lying on the ground. When he saw the boy he got up, thinking that perhaps he would at least be moved to a different place.

But the young peasant did not even touch the wooden hammer he used for moving the post. Instead he came close, stared at the animal, and threw at the horse a lump of earth which broke up when it struck his white old head. Then he walked away, whistling a tune.

The horse managed to stay on his feet as long as the boy was in sight, then, knowing that it would be useless to at-

**neigh,* sound made by a horse.
**torture,* to cause pain.

tempt to reach the grass, he lay down again on his side and closed his eyes.

The next day Zidore did not turn up.

The horse is dead

When he came the following day and went up to Coco, who was still lying on his side, he saw that the horse was dead.

He stood there, looking down at him, very pleased with what he had done, even though he was surprised that it had happened so quickly. He touched the horse with his foot, then lifted up one of the animal's legs, let it drop again and finally sat down on the body, staring at the grass for a while, his mind a blank.

When he returned to the farm he said nothing about what had happened, because he wanted to make sure he would still be free to wander through the woods during the period when he was supposed to be looking after the horse.

He went out to see him the next day. As he approached, a few crows flew away from the dead body. Thousands of flies were crawling all over it, and flying round it.

When he got back to the farm he told them. As the animal was so old nobody was in the least surprised. The farmer said to two of his men, 'Get your shovels. You'd better dig a hole and bury him just where he's lying.'

And the men buried the horse in the very place where he had died of hunger.

The grass there grew thick and tall, fed by his poor old body.

10 He?

My dear friend, you are completely puzzled by it, aren't you? And I can easily understand why. I suppose you think I've gone mad. Perhaps I am a little mad, but not for the reason you imagine.

Yes. In spite of all I've said, I'm getting married. It's quite true.

As a matter of fact I hardly know the girl who will become my wife tomorrow. I have only seen her four or five times. I know that I find her quite pleasant, and this is enough for my purpose.

She is not rich. She comes from an ordinary family. She is the sort of girl you can find by the hundred. She belongs to that great number of nice ordinary girls, whom you think you are glad you married – until the day when you discover that, in fact, you prefer all the other women to the one you have chosen.

'Then why on earth are you marrying her?' you will say.

I hardly dare tell you the strange incredible reason which is urging me to perform this senseless action.

I am getting married so I shall not have to be alone!

I don't know how to tell you about it, how to make myself understood. I am in such a miserable state of mind that you will feel sorry for me, and also perhaps be scornful.

I cannot bear to be alone any more at night. I want to feel some human near me, touching me, a human person who can speak, say something, anything at all.

I want to be able to wake her up, suddenly ask her a question of some kind, even a silly question – just so I can hear a voice. I want to feel that my home is lived in, feel that there is another soul awake, in the house. I want to see, when I quickly light the candle by my bed, another human face next to mine because, you see, I am afraid of being on my own. I'm so ashamed I hardly dare admit it.

Oh, I don't suppose you will understand!

It's not that I'm afraid of any danger. If a thief came into the room I would kill him without the slightest fear. I'm not afraid of ghosts and I'm not afraid of the dead.

I am afraid of myself

'Well, then!' you'll say. 'What are you afraid of?' Well, I'm afraid of myself! I'm afraid of fear, afraid of that dreadful feeling of horror which I cannot explain.

Oh, you can laugh, if you like. But it's terrible, and I can't stop it. I'm afraid of the walls, of the furniture, of familiar objects, which seem to me to take on a kind of animal life. Above all I am afraid of the terrible confusion of my thoughts, of the way I am so filled with fear that I cannot think clearly.

At first I feel a vague nervousness which enters my soul and makes me tremble all over. I look all round me. There's nothing there. And yet I wish there were something there to be seen, something I could understand. The only reason I'm frightened is that I don't understand the cause of my fear.

I happen to say something aloud – and I'm frightened by the sound of my own voice! I walk about my room, and I'm afraid there might be something strange behind the door, behind the curtains in the cupboard, under my bed. And yet I know very well that there is nothing there at all.

Sometimes I suddenly turn round because I'm afraid of what might be behind me – and yet there is nothing there, as I very well know.

I feel the nervousness increasing, and so I lock myself in my room, bury myself in my bed and hide under the sheets. Then I close my eyes in despair, and stay like this for a long, long time, knowing full well that my candle is still burning on the bed-side table, and that I really ought to put it out. Yet I haven't the courage to do so!

Isn't it dreadful, to be in this state?

I never used to feel in the least like this. I used to come home calm and cheerful. I used to walk around my flat without anything disturbing me. If somebody had told me that one day I should be attacked by silly, senseless, terror, I would have laughed at him. When it was dark I was never nervous when I opened doors. I used to take my time going to bed, and I never bothered to lock the doors and windows. I never used to get up in the middle of the night, as I do now, to make sure that everything was properly fastened.

How did my fear start?

It all started last year in a very curious way. It was one damp evening in autumn. I had finished dinner, the servant had left the flat, and I was wondering what I could do to pass the time. For a while I walked up and down my room. I was feeling very tired for no particular reason. I felt completely unable to work, and had not even the energy to read a book. The windows were wet with a fine rain. I felt so unhappy I could have cried. I wanted to talk to somebody, anybody at all, just to shake off the heavy sadness of my thoughts.

I was feeling very lonely. My flat seemed emptier than it had ever been before. I felt as though I was drowning in a loneliness that would never end. What could I do? I sat down, and then felt a kind of nervous eagerness seize my legs. I stood up and started to walk up and down the room again. I certainly had a slight fever. I was holding my hands behind my back – in the way you often do when you are walking slowly up and down. I noticed that they felt hot to the touch. Then, suddenly, a shiver ran down my back. It struck me that the damp night air might be getting into my room, and I thought I would light a fire. I did so. It was the first I had lit that autumn. And I sat down once again, watching the flames. Soon, however, the feeling that I could not possibly sit still got me to my feet again, and I knew that I would have to get out, shake off my sadness, find a friend to talk to.

I went out. I called to see three of my friends, but not one of them was at home. Then I went as far as the main streets, determined to find somebody I knew.

Everywhere was miserable. The damp pavements were

gleaming in the gaslight. The mild, wet air was lying heavily over the streets, where it seemed to tire the weak flames of the gas lamps.

I walked on slowly, saying to myself, 'I shan't find anybody I can talk to.'

Several times I looked into cafés. Sad-looking people were sitting at tables, looking as though they had not even the strength to finish their drinks.

I wandered about like this for a long time, and towards midnight I set off back home. I was very calm now, but very tired. My caretaker, who is usually in bed by eleven o'clock, opened the door straight away. This was not what I would have expected, and I thought, 'Hello! It looks as though another person has just gone upstairs ahead of me.'

Now, when I go out I always make sure my door is locked. When I got up to my flat I found that the door was only pulled to, and this struck me as rather strange. I thought that perhaps the caretaker had brought a letter up to my room during the evening.

Someone was sitting in my chair

I entered my flat. The fire was still alight, and was even burning enough to light up the room a little. I picked up a candle with the intention of lighting it at the fire, when, looking straight ahead, I noticed somebody sitting in my fireside chair, warming his feet, with his back towards me.

I was not at all frightened. A very likely explanation immediately came to me. It looked as though one of my friends had come to see me. The caretaker, to whom I had spoken on my way out, had told him I would be coming back and had lent him a key. And in a flash I remembered the things I had noticed on my return: the fact that the street-door was opened immediately, and that my own door was not locked.

I could only see the back of my friend's head. He had evidently fallen asleep in front of the fire while waiting for me, so I went across in order to wake him. I could see him perfectly clearly. His right arm was hanging down, and his

legs were crossed. His head, leaning back on the chair, a little to the left, gave a clear picture of a man asleep.

I asked myself, 'Who can it be?' There was not much light in the room, and I still could not see who he was. So I stretched out my hand to touch him on the shoulder.

My hand came into contact with the wood of the chair-back! There was no longer anybody sitting there! The chair was empty!

My God! How I jumped!

Instantly I drew back as though there was some terrible danger.

Then I turned round, feeling sure that there was somebody standing behind me. Then immediately feeling an urgent need to see the chair again, I spun round on my heels. I stood there, breathing fast in terror, so amazed that I could no longer think, so shaken that I was ready to drop.

But I am normally a man with self-control, and I soon recovered. I thought, 'I've just experienced some kind of hallucination* that's all.' And I immediately began to think of how this could have happened. Thoughts move very quickly in such moments as this.

I had experienced an hallucination. That was a fact I could not deny. Now, during this experience my mind had remained absolutely clear, working quite normally. So there was no confusion caused by the working of my brain. It was only my eyes that had been deceived, or rather, they had deceived my mind. What had happened was that there had been some kind of disturbance of the nerves to my eyes. My eyes were probably just tired.

So I lit my candle. As I bent down towards the fire I noticed that I was trembling. I stood up again very rapidly, as though somebody had touched me from behind.

I had not been able to calm myself, that was certain. I walked about a while, talked in a loud voice, and sang a few tunes.

Then I locked my door and this made me a little less anxious. Anyhow nobody could get in.

**hallucination,* something seen which is not real.

I sat down, and for a long time I thought about what I had experienced. Then I went to bed and blew out my candle.

He was still there

For a few minutes all was well. I was lying on my back, feeling quite calm. Then I felt I simply had to look across the room, and I turned over on my side.

All that remained of my fire was a few glowing pieces of coal, the light which faintly lit up the legs of my fire-side chair in which I thought I saw the man sitting again.

With a rapid movement I struck a match. I had been mistaken. There was nothing to be seen.

I got up, however, and went and hid the chair behind my bed.

Then I blew out my candle again, and tried to get to sleep. I had not been asleep for more than five minutes when I dreamt that I saw the whole thing again, as clearly as if it was real. I woke up in a state of terror and having lit the candle, I stayed there, sitting up in bed, without even daring to try to get to sleep again.

Twice, however, I was overcome by sleep in spite of myself, just for a few moments. And twice I saw the thing again. I thought I was going mad.

As soon as daylight appeared I felt that I was cured, and I slept peacefully until noon.

It was all over, completely finished. I had been feverish, had a nightmare, or something of that sort. I had been ill, in fact. Even so, I felt that I had made a real fool of myself.

The next evening

I was very cheerful that day. In the evening I went out for a meal, and afterwards went to the theatre. I set off to walk back home, but as I got near the house I was overcome by a strange uneasiness. I was afraid of seeing 'him' again. I was not actually afraid of 'him', not afraid of his presence, in which I simply did not believe, but I was afraid that my eyes might play tricks on me again, afraid of another hallucination, afraid of the terror which would then come upon me.

For more than an hour I walked up and down the pavement in front of the house. Then I eventually decided that my behaviour really was too ridiculous for words, and I went in.

I was so short of breath that I could hardly get up the stairs, and stood for another ten minutes waiting on the landing outside my flat. Then, suddenly, my courage came back. I pushed my key into the key-hole, and rushed in with a candle in my hand. I kicked open the inner door which was standing ajar and took a terrified glance at the fire-place. There was nothing to be seen. Ah! What a relief! What a delight! I walked about the room cheerfully and confidently. Yet I was not entirely satisfied. I kept turning round. I was bothered by the shadows in corners of my room.

I did not sleep very well, and was constantly waking up because I imagined I heard something. But I did not see 'him'. It was all over!

I can't forget him

Ever since that time I have been afraid when I have been alone at night. I feel that it's there, quite near me, round about me, this ghost. It has not appeared to me again. Oh, no! And, in any case, even if it did, what does it matter? I don't believe in it. I know that it doesn't exist.

Yet it still bothers me, because I am constantly thinking about it. His right arm was hanging down, his head was leaning to the left, just like the head of a man asleep. Oh, stop it! I don't want to think about it any more!

And yet why am I always thinking about this thing? Why is memory always there? His feet were quite close to the fire!

He is haunting me. I know it sounds mad, but that's the way it is. Who is haunting me? 'He'? I know very well that 'he' doesn't exist, that there is nothing there! He only exists in my nervous imagination, in my fear, in my terror. Oh, I must stop talking about it like this!

Yes, but however hard I try to argue myself out of it and strengthen my courage, I can no longer stay at home on my own, because 'he' is there. I shall not see him again, I know.

He won't show himself again, that's all over. But he is there all the same, in my thoughts. Even though he cannot be seen that does not prevent him from being there. He is behind the doors, in the cupboard, under the bed, in all the dark corners, in every shadow. If I open the door, if I open the cupboard, if I take a candle and look under the bed, if I light up the shadowy corners, he is no longer there. But then I sense that he is behind me and I turn round, though I am sure that I shall not see him, that I will never see him again. Nevertheless, he is behind me, still behind me.

It's stupid, but it's frightening. I'm sorry, I simply can't help it.

But if there were two of us in my flat, I feel absolutely certain that he wouldn't be there any more. You see, he's there because I am alone. Just because I am alone.

11 A Duel

The war of 1870 was over. Prussia had conquered France and there were German soldiers everywhere. The first trains were now able to leave Paris, and they were slowly passing through the country, where the passengers could see from the windows the villages that had been burnt and destroyed. In front of the buildings that were still standing they could see Prussian soldiers wearing their black helmets* with gleaming brass points. They were smoking their pipes, sitting on chairs and talking cheerfully to each other as if they were at home in their own country. When the trains passed through a town the passengers could see the soldiers marching, and above the noise made by the train they occasionally heard the shouts of the officers as they gave their commands.

Mr Dubuis had been in the national guard which had defended Paris. Now he was travelling to Switzerland to join his wife and daughter, whom he had sent there for safety just before France had been invaded. In spite of the shortage of food and all the difficulties caused by the war he still had the fat stomach of a wealthy, peace-loving businessman. He had taken very calmly all the terrible things he had suffered but he had said hard things about the savage behaviour of men. Now that the war was over and he was getting near to the frontier he could see Prussian soldiers for the first time. He had done his duty and helped to guard Paris on many cold nights, but this was the first time he had actually seen the enemy soldiers.

He looked at them with a mixture of fear and anger, these men with guns and beards who were settling down on French soil, just as if this was their home country. He felt in his soul a kind of fever, because he loved his country so much, and yet he was weak and helpless. He also felt the need to behave with extreme care.

**helmet,* a kind of hat which protects the head.

Sitting with him in the same compartment* were two Englishmen. They were tourists and now that the war was over they had come to see France for themselves. They looked out of the window with their calm, inquiring eyes. Like Monsieur Dubuis they were both fat, and they were talking to each other in English, occasionally looking in their guide-book and reading aloud the names of the places they were trying to recognise.

The Prussian officer

The train stopped at the station of a small town. A Prussian officer got into the compartment, making a great noise as his sword banged against the steps. He was tall, with a big beard, and he was dressed in a tightly fitting uniform. His beard and hair were so red that they seemed to be on fire, and his big moustache*, which was a little paler, stuck out at both sides of his face.

The Englishmen immediately looked at him, smiling because their curiosity was satisfied. Here was a real Prussian officer. Mr Dubuis pretended to read his newspaper. He sat deep in the corner of the compartment like a criminal sitting opposite a policeman.

The train set off, and the two Englishmen started talking again, trying to recognise the places where the battles had taken place. Suddenly, as one of them was pointing out of the window, the Prussian officer leaned backwards, stretched out his legs, and said, 'I killed twelve Frenchmen in that village. I took more than a hundred prisoners.'

The English tourists, very interested, asked him, 'Oh! And what's it called, that village?'

'Pharsbourg,' replied the Prussian. 'I had those French pigs by the ears!'

And he looked at Mr Dubuis and laughed proudly, deep in his beard.

The train travelled on. They could see German soldiers everywhere, along the roads, in the fields, standing by gates,

*compartment, part of a train.
*moustache, hair growing above the mouth.

Théatres à
Le Casino

sitting outside cafés. They seemed to cover the ground like insects.

'If I had been in command,' said the officer, stretching out his arms, 'I'd have captured Paris, and I'd have burnt everything and killed everybody. There'd have been no more France!'

'Oh, yes,' replied the Englishmen politely.

'In twenty years,' continued the officer, 'the whole of Europe will belong to us! All of it! Prussia is stronger than all the countries in the world.'

The Englishmen, looking rather worried, did not reply. The Prussian now started to laugh. Still leaning back on his seat he made fun of the French, pouring terrible insults on his enemies. He made fun of Austria, which Prussia had recently conquered. He made fun of the fierce but hopeless defence put up by the French army. He announced that Bismark was going to build an iron city with all the guns he had captured.

Suddenly he stuck out his feet and rested his boots on the Frenchman's knees. Mr Dubuis turned his head away, his face red from ear to ear.

The Englishmen looked as if they were not really interested. It was as though they were shut up in their island, safe from the noisy world outside.

The officer took out his pipe, and staring hard at the Frenchmen he said, 'I don't suppose you've any tobacco?'

'No, sir,' replied Mr Dubuis.

'When the train stops,' said the German, 'I want you to go and get me some.'

Then he started laughing again and said, 'I'll give you a tip!'

The train whistled and began to slow down. They passed the station buildings which had been damaged by fire, then stopped.

The German opened the door and seized Mr Dubuis by the arm.

'Off you go and get that tobacco for me!' he said. 'Quickly! Quickly!'

Dubuis escapes

The station was full of Prussian soldiers standing all along the platform. The engine gave another whistle, already setting off again. Suddenly, Mr Dubuis jumped down onto the platform and, in spite of the guard waving at him, he quickly got into the next compartment.

He was alone! His heart was beating so fast that he had to open his waistcoat. He wiped the sweat from his forehead and sat there, breathing hard.

The train came to another station and stopped once again. Suddenly the officer appeared at the door of the compartment and he got in, followed by the two English tourists who were curious to see what would happen.

The German sat down opposite the Frenchman and, still laughing, he said, 'So you wouldn't get the tobacco for me!'

'No, sir!' replied Mr Dubuis.

The train had just set off again when the officer said, 'I'm going to cut off your moustache and fill my pipe with that!'

And he stretched out his hand towards the Frenchman's face. The two Englishmen, still showing no excitement, looked on steadily. The German had already taken hold of a few hairs between his fingers and was pulling hard, when Mr Dubuis knocked away his arm with the back of his hand. Seizing the Prussian by the collar he threw him back into his seat. Then, crazy with anger, and with staring eyes and the veins standing out on his forehead, he held the officer's throat with one hand and with the other started hitting him violently in the face.

Dubuis nearly kills the Prussian

The Prussian struggled, trying to get his sword out, trying to get hold of the enemy who was lying on top of him. But Mr Dubuis was crushing him with the weight of his enormous stomach, and he kept on hitting him, hitting away without stopping, without waiting to get his breath back, without even knowing where the blows fell.

Blood was flowing now. The German, choking, struggling

to breathe, spitting out broken teeth, tried in vain to push away this angry fat man who was killing him.

The English tourists had got up and come nearer so they could get a better view. They stood there delighted, curious to see who would win the fight.

Suddenly, Mr Dubuis, worn out by such a great effort, stopped hitting the officer and sat down again without saying a word.

The Prussian was so frightened, so full of amazement, and in such pain, that he did not move. When he had got his breath back he said, 'You will fight a duel with me, with pistols! If you refuse, then I'll kill you straight away!'

'Whenever you want,' replied Mr Dubuis. 'I'd be glad to!'

'We're entering the city of Strasbourg,' said the German. 'I'll find two officers to act as my seconds. There'll just be time to fight a duel before the train leaves.'

Mr Dubuis, who was breathing so hard he was making as much noise as the engine, turned to the Englishmen and said, 'Will you act as my seconds?'

'Oh, yes!' they replied, speaking at the same time.

The train stopped. Within a minute the Prussian had found two friends, who brought him a pair of pistols. Then they all went a short distance out of the city. The Englishmen kept taking their watches out and hurrying everybody along. They were worried about the time, afraid they might not get back before the train left.

Mr Dubuis had never held a pistol in his life. They made him stand twenty yards from his enemy, then asked him, 'Are you ready?'

'Yes, sir,' he replied. He noticed that one of the Englishmen had opened his umbrella to shade himself from the hot sun.

A voice shouted out, 'Fire!'

The Prussian dies

Mr Dubuis fired, without waiting, and without taking proper aim. In amazement he saw the Prussian start to sway, then fall flat on his face. He had killed him.

'Oh!' said one of the Englishmen in a voice trembling with delight, his curiosity now completely satisfied. The other Englishman, still looking at his watch, seized Mr Dubuis by the arm and dragged him off to the station as fast as they could go.

'One, two! One, two!' called out the first Englishman, marking time as they ran, with his fingers tightly closed and his elbows close to his sides. And all three of them galloped along, in spite of their enormous stomachs, looking like three funny men in a children's picture book.

The train was leaving the station. They jumped into a compartment. Then the Englishmen took off their hats and waved them in the air, shouting three times, 'Hip, hip, hurrah!'

Very seriously, they both shook hands with Mr Dubuis, then went to sit in their corner.

12 Who Knows?

At last I am going to put down in writing all that has happened to me! But how can I do it? How dare I do it? It's all so strange, so hard to understand, so crazy!

If I were not certain about what I have seen, certain that I have made no mistakes in any of my observations, I would think that I was just the victim of some trick of the imagination. After all, who knows?

I am writing this in a private mental hospital. But I have come in here of my own free will, because I am afraid. Only one living person knows my story – the doctor in charge here. And now I am going to write it down, I don't really know why. Perhaps it is so I can get it out of my system, for I can feel it constantly rising inside me, like some awful nightmare. Well, here it is.

I have always lived alone, because I feel very nervous when I am with other people. How can I explain this? I don't think I can explain it. It's not that I refuse to see people, or to talk to them, or to have dinner with friends. But when I've been with them for some time, even with the people I know best, I find that they tire me out, make me nervous. I want to see them go, or go away myself, so that I can be alone.

I am so fond of being all alone that I can't even bear to have other people sleeping under the same roof. I can't bear to live in Paris because, for me, it seems like a slow death. I find that my body and nerves are hurt by the great crowds of people who are living all round me, even when they are asleep.

Why do I feel like this? Who knows? Perhaps there is a very simple explanation. It may be because I soon get tired of anything which takes place outside of me.

One of the results of all this is that I become very fond of the objects in my house which seem to me to be as important as living creatures. My house has become – or rather, *had* become – a whole world in which I lived a lonely yet busy life, surrounded by the familiar pieces of furniture and other possessions, which seemed to me to be as warm and friendly as human faces. I had gradually filled my home with these things, and when I was safe inside I felt content and happy.

This house stood in a beautiful garden which separated it from the roads. But it was within reach of a town where, if I wanted to, I could find all the activities in which I sometimes took an interest. All my servants slept in a building some distance away at the bottom of the garden, which was surrounded by a high wall.

I return home late one evening

On that particular evening I had been to the theatre in town. I was walking back home, feeling very cheerful because I was going to be all alone again. It was so dark that I could hardly see the edge of the main road, and several times I nearly fell into a ditch. The distance I had to walk to my house was about a mile, perhaps a little more. It was about one o'clock in the morning, possibly as late as half past one. As I walked, the sky ahead of me seemed to grow a little lighter, and a thin moon appeared, shining very sadly, so pale that it made no shadows. In the distance I could see the dark group of trees which surrounded my garden, and for some reason I felt nervous at the thought of entering it. I started to walk more slowly. The night was very mild.

I opened my gate and walked down the long avenue of trees which led up to the house. The branches made an arch above me, so that it was like walking through a dark tunnel.

When I got near the house I felt strangely disturbed. I stood still. There was not a sound to be heard. There was not a leaf moving in the breeze. 'What is the matter with me?' I thought. For ten years I had been coming home like this without feeling the slightest bit of nervousness. I was not afraid, and I never have been afraid, when coming home late at night. If I had seen a stranger, a thief perhaps, I would have leaped on him angrily, without hesitating. Besides, I was armed. I had my revolver with me. Why was I so nervous?

As I moved slowly forwards I had a strange, cold feeling all over my skin. When I got to the wall of my big house, I knew that I would have to wait a few minutes before I could open the door and go inside. So I sat down on a seat under the windows of my sitting-room. I stayed there for a while, trembling a little, with my head leaning back against the wall of the house, and my eyes wide open, staring at the dark trees. For the first few moments I noticed nothing unusual. There was a sort of rushing sound in my ears, but I often get that. It sometimes seems as though I can hear trains going by, or bells ringing, or marching footsteps.

The noise is coming from the house

But soon these head noises became louder, clearer. I had been mistaken. It was not the usual rushing of blood that was filling my ears with this sound, but a very peculiar, rather confused noise. There was no doubt whatever that it was coming from inside my house.

Through the wall I could hear this continuous noise – a sort of confused sound you would expect if a number of things were being moved about. It was as though all my pieces of furniture were trembling and being moved from their accustomed places, being gently dragged about the house.

Oh, I can assure you that for a few moments I doubted the evidence of my senses. But when I had pressed my ear against a window so I could get a better idea of what was going on inside, I became absolutely certain that in my home something was taking place which was impossible to understand. I was not exactly afraid. I was so full of amazement. I didn't even take out my revolver, because I felt sure there would be no need to use it. I simply waited.

I waited for a long time, unable to come to any decision, thinking very clearly, but weak with nervousness. I waited, standing there, listening all the time to the noise which was now growing louder, occasionally reaching a kind of violent height, which seemed like a growl of anger.

Then, suddenly feeling ashamed of my cowardice, I took my bunch of keys and found the one I needed. I pushed it into the key-hole, turned it in the lock, and pushing on the door with all my strength I swung it open so violently that it banged against the wall inside.

The noise it made rang out like a gun being fired. Instantly, as if in reply to this loud bang, from the whole of my house, from top to bottom, there came the most enormous roar. It came as such a shock, with such horror, and was so deafening, that I took a few steps backwards. Though I still knew it was useless, I took out my revolver.

The furniture marches out of the house

I waited, but not for long! Now I could hear an extraordinary stamping noise on the stairs, on the floors, on the carpets – not stamping of shoes worn by humans, but the stamping of crutches* – wooden crutches, and iron crutches which made a terrible noise. And then I suddenly noticed an armchair on my front door-step, the big armchair I always used when reading. It was going out of the house, swaying as it went. It was going off into the garden. Other chairs followed it, the ones out of my sitting-room. Then out came all the rest of my chairs, leaping about like goats, and the little stools, leaping along like rabbits.

What a state I was in! I ran out and hid in the bushes, unable to take my eyes off this march-past of my furniture. Every piece of it was going, one article after the other, some quickly, some slowly, depending on the size and weight. My huge piano galloped past like a run-away horse, rattling with music. The tiniest little objects were running down the avenue like ants, even the glasses in which the moonlight shone with a strange gleam. The curtains and carpets were moving along like slippery creatures from the sea. Then I saw my writing-desk appear. It was a very valuable antique* and

**crutches,* kind of sticks to help people to walk.
**antique,* old piece of furniture.

it contained all the letters I have ever received, the entire story of my personal life, a long story which has brought me so much suffering! And there were photographs in there, too.

Suddenly, I was afraid no longer. I rushed forward and flung myself on this desk, taking hold of it as if I were stopping a thief. But it continued fiercely on its way, and in spite of all my struggles and anger, I could not even manage to slow it down. Struggling like a desperate man against this terrible strength, I was thrown to the ground still trying to hold it back. Then it sent me rolling over, dragged me along the avenue. The furniture that had been coming along behind it started to walk over me, stamping on my legs and hurting me badly. Then, as soon as I had let go of the desk, the rest of the furniture passed over my body, just like soldiers charging over an enemy who had fallen from his horse.

The house is completely empty

By this time I was mad with terror, but I managed to drag myself out of the avenue and hide once again amongst the trees. From there I watched all my possessions disappearing into the night – every single one of them – the smallest, the most ordinary, even the ones I had never paid much attention to, but all of them belonging to me.

Then I heard, some distance away, the great banging of doors being shut. It came from my own home which was now filled with the loud echoes of an empty house. The doors of the building banged shut from top to bottom, until finally, the front door banged shut last of all, behind my escaping furniture.

I also made my escape, running all the way to the town, and I only recovered when I got into the streets where there were a few people about, coming home late. I went and rang at the door of a hotel where I was well-known. With my hands I had rubbed the dirt off my clothes, and I told the hotel manager that I had lost my bunch of keys. This included the key to the garden gate where my servants lived in a building separated from my house by the high wall.

They gave me a bed, and though I hid myself under the

sheets I couldn't sleep, but lay there waiting for dawn, listening to the beating of my heart. I had told somebody in the hotel to tell my servant where I was as soon as it was light. At seven o'clock in the morning my servant Philippe banged on my door. From his face I could see that he was terribly upset.

'Something dreadful has happened during the night, sir,' he said.

'What do you mean?'

'All your furniture has been stolen, sir, everything, absolutely everything, even down to the smallest articles.'

I felt pleased when I heard him say this. Why? Who knows? I was completely in control of myself, certain that I would be able to hide my feelings and not tell anybody about what I I had seen, certain that I could hide this thing, bury it deep in my mind like some dreadful secret. I answered him by saying, 'It must be the people who stole my keys. We must inform the police immediately. I'll get dressed and be with you in just a few moments.'

The inquiry went on for five months. The police discovered nothing whatever. They could not find the smallest of my possessions, nor discover the slightest detail about the thieves. My God! If I had told them what I knew, they would have locked *me* up, not the thieves.

Oh, I knew how to keep my mouth shut. But I didn't start putting new furniture into my house. It would have been quite useless. The whole thing would have started all over again. I didn't want to go back to my house. I never did go back. I never saw it again.

I came to Paris and stayed in a hotel. I saw various doctors about the state of my nerves, something which has been worrying me a good deal ever since that terrible night.

They strongly advised me to travel. I took their advice.

A visit to Rouen

I began with a trip to Italy. The sunshine there did me good. Then I travelled through Sicily, an island which has wonderful scenery. I went over to Africa, and made a safe journey across that great, calm, yellow desert, where the air is so bright and clear that you never think of ghosts and the horror of darkness.

I returned to France by way of Marseilles. The fact that the skies were less bright than in Africa made me rather sad. On returning to Europe I felt as a sick man must feel when he believes himself to be cured, and then a pain reminds him that the disease is still there.

I came back to Paris, and after a month here, I became bored. By now it was autumn, and before winter started I wanted to take a trip through Normandy, where I had never been before.

I began by visiting Rouen, of course, and for a whole week I wandered in a state of delight through this ancient city, with its amazing streets and extraordinary old buildings.

One afternoon, about four o'clock, I turned down a most peculiar street, along which flowed a stream as black as ink. I was gazing up at the strange, old houses, when my attention was suddenly caught by the sight of a whole row of shops dealing in second-hand furniture.

How well these men who sold antiques had chosen their position. There they were in this mysterious street, above this evil-looking stream, and above them were the pointed roofs which seemed to creak with old age.

In the depths of these dark shops you could see an untidy mixture of furniture, pots, ornaments, pictures, statues of Jesus, Mary and the saints. Oh, what strange caves there were in these tall houses, full from cellar to roof-top with objects of every possible kind. They were objects whose life seemed to be over and yet which had lived longer than their owners, even longer than their century and their fashion.

My interest in antiques was awakened again in this mysterious street. I went from shop to shop, taking quick light steps across the little bridges made from three or four rotten boards which lay across the evil-smelling water of the stream.

I find my furniture again

What a shock! I found myself looking at one of my own

cupboards, one of the finest I had. It was standing at the side of a room full of antiques, a place which looked like the entrance to a graveyard for old furniture. I went up to the cupboard, trembling all over, trembling so much that I hardly dared touch it. Hesitating, I reached out my hand. Yes! It really was mine, a remarkable antique from the period of Louis XIII which would have been recognised immediately by anyone who had seen it even once. Suddenly looking a little further into the darkness of the room, I noticed three of my own armchairs. Then, still further in, I saw my antique tables from the Henry II period. They were so rare that people used to come all the way from Paris to see them.

Just imagine how I felt! Just think of my state of mind!

I moved further into the shop. I was nearly sick with fear, but I am not a coward, and in spite of my terror I moved forward, feeling as though I was entering a place of mysterious evil. I went on, and at each step I took I found something that had belonged to me – my candle-sticks, my books, my pictures, my curtains, my antique weapons. Everything was there except the writing-desk containing my letters, and this was nowhere to be seen.

I went on, going down steps leading to lower floors, then climbing to ones higher up. I was all alone. I called out, but nobody answered. I was all alone, there was not another soul in this great building.

Night came, and I had to sit there in the darkness on one of my own chairs for I had made up my mind that I would not leave the place. Every now and then I shouted out, 'Hello! Hello! Is anybody there?'

I must have been there for more than an hour when I heard the sound of light, slow footsteps coming from somewhere just above me. I nearly jumped up and ran out into the street, but, steadying myself, I called out once again. Then I saw a light appear in a room just above me.

The man in the shop

'Who's there?' asked a voice.

'A customer,' I replied.

The answer came back, 'It's very late for you to be coming into a shop, isn't it?'

'I've been waiting for you for more than an hour,' I answered.

'You could come back tomorrow.'

'Tomorrow I shall have left Rouen.'

I simply dared not go towards him, and he was not coming out to me. The bright glow was still coming from his lamp and lighting up an antique curtain. This article, too, belonged to me.

I called out, 'Well, then? Are you coming out?'

He replied, 'I'm waiting for you.'

I got up and went towards him.

In the middle of a large room there stood a little man, very short and so fat that he was like some ugly monster.

He had a thin, untidy beard, which was yellow in patches, and there was not a hair on his head! Not a hair! As he lifted up his candle at arm's length so he could see me better, his head looked just like a little round moon in this enormous room full of old furniture. His face looked as though it was swollen and his eyes were so deep I could hardly see them.

I bargained with him for three chairs which belonged to me, and paid him a large sum for them in cash, giving him only the number of my room and the name of the hotel. The chairs were to be delivered the following morning by nine o'clock.

Then I left. He saw me to the door, behaving very politely.

I go to the police

I then went to the police and told them about how my furniture had been stolen and what I had just discovered.

The police officer immediately sent a telegram to the department which had been making enquiries about my missing furniture. He asked me to wait until he received the information he required. An hour later the reply came, proving that I had told the truth about what was missing.

'I'm going to have this man arrested and questioned,' said the police officer. 'And it must be done immediately, because he might have got suspicious and had your property moved. If you can go and have a meal and come back in two hours, I'll have him here by then and I can question him again in your presence.'

'I can certainly do that. I am extremely grateful to you.'

I went to my hotel and had a dinner which I enjoyed so much I hardly believed it possible. I suppose I was feeling very pleased about the way things had worked out. At last we had him.

Two hours later I went back to the police officer, who was waiting for me.

'Well, now, sir!' he said as soon as he saw me. 'We've not found this thief of yours. My men haven't been able to get their hands on him at all.'

'Ah!' I said, and suddenly felt as though I was going to faint.

'But,' I asked him, 'surely you've managed to find his house?'

'Yes, indeed. And I'm going to have my men watch it until he gets back. But as for the man himself, he's disappeared!'

'Disappeared?'

'Yes, disappeared. He usually spends his evenings at the house of a neighbour, a woman who is a second-hand dealer, like himself – a strange old woman, a widow by the name of Bidoin. She hasn't seen him tonight, and she can't tell us where he is. We shall have to wait until tomorrow.'

I left the police-station. Ah, those ancient streets of Rouen, how evil, how disturbing, how haunted they now seemed to me!

I slept very badly that night, with a nightmare at the end of each short period of sleep.

The next day I waited until ten o'clock before going to the police. I didn't want to give them the idea that I was too anxious or too much in a hurry.

The dealer had not turned up. His shop was still closed.

The police officer said to me, 'I've done everything that was necessary. I've contacted headquarters. I want you to come with us to this shop. I'll have it forced open, and then you can show me what belongs to you.'

When we arrived, policemen were standing in front of the shop and we soon broke open the door.

When I went in I could see neither my cupboard, nor my armchairs, nor my tables, nor any of the furniture that had once been in my house – nothing whatever. Yet the night before I could hardly move a step without coming across something of mine.

The police officer was surprised, and at first he looked at me rather suspiciously.

I said, 'My word, sir, it's remarkable that the furniture has disappeared at the same time as the dealer.'

'That's certainly true,' he said, with a smile. 'You know, you were wrong to buy those things of yours yesterday, and pay for them as well. It'll have made him suspicious.'

'What I simply can't understand,' I said, 'is that every single space that was taken by my furniture has now been filled by other articles.'

'Oh,' replied the superintendent, 'he's had all night, and probably had some help as well. Don't worry, sir. I'm going to give this case my personal attention. Now we know his hiding-place, it won't be long before we get our hands on this criminal.'

Ah, my heart, my heart, my poor heart, how it was beating!

The furniture returns to my house

I stayed in Rouen for two weeks. The man never came back.

Now, on the morning of the fifteenth day I received from the gardener who had been left in charge of my empty house the following strange letter,

Dear Sir,

I am writing to inform you that last night something happened which none of us can understand, not even the police. All the furniture has come back – all of it, with not a single thing missing. It's all here, down to the tiniest little things. The house is now exactly the same as it was on the night the furniture was stolen. It's enough to drive you mad. It happened in the middle of the night, between Friday and Saturday. The whole avenue has got deep marks in it, and it looks as though they'd dragged everything from the gate right up to the front door. It was just like this the day everything disappeared.

We're waiting for you to come back, sir, and I remain

Your obedient servant,

Philippe.

Oh no! No! No! No! I shall never go back.

I took this letter to the police officer in Rouen. 'He's been clever enough to take it all back,' he said. 'Don't worry, we'll catch this man one of these days.'

I decide to hide

But they haven't caught him. Oh, no. They haven't caught him – and I'm as afraid of him now as if he were a fierce animal about to leap on me from behind my back.

They'll never find him. Never. Nobody can possibly find him, this monster with the head like a moon. They'll never catch him. He'll never go back to his shop. What does *he* care? I am the only person who could possibly recognise him, and I don't want to!

And, anyhow, what if he does come back, what if he does return to his shop, who will be able to prove that my furniture was there? Mine is the only evidence against him, and I know very well that the police are beginning to be suspicious of me.

Oh, no! I couldn't go on living that kind of a life. And yet I couldn't keep quiet about what I have seen. I couldn't go on living a normal life as long as I feared the possibility of this business starting all over again.

So I came to see the doctor who runs this private mental hospital, and I told him everything.

After he had spent a long time asking me questions, he said, 'Would you be willing to stay here for a while?'

'Yes, I'd be glad to.'

'Have you enough money?'

'Yes.'

'Would you like private rooms?'

'Yes.'

'Would you like any of your friends to come and visit you?'

'No! I don't want anybody! The man from Rouen might try to get at me here, out of revenge.'

And I have been alone, all alone, for three months. My nerves are more or less calm now. I have just one fear. Suppose the antique-dealer went mad and suppose they brought him into this place. Even the prisons are not safe.

Questions

A Night of Terror

1. What are the first signs that the fisherman is nervous?
2. Give two reasons why he could not get the boat free.
3. Why does the thick, white mist make him even more afraid?
4. Why does he decide not to swim to the river bank?
5. At what point in the story does he stop being afraid – and why?
6. Did the ending come as a surprise to you? Do you think the fisherman had somehow sensed that the body was there?

The Hand

1. What remark does the writer make about women? Do you agree with him?
2. Explain the meaning of the word 'vendetta'.
3. How does the judge get to know the mysterious Englishman?
4. When the Englishman says that the hand needs to be chained to the wall, what two explanations does the judge give for his strange remark?
5. How do we know that the Englishman is living in fear?
6. After the murder, what makes the judge look to see if the hand is still here?
7. What is there about the hand which shows that it must have been connected with the murder?
8. The women do not accept the judge's explanation. Do you?

A Coward

1. Give an example of the way Signoles used to boast.
2. Why did he strike the man across the face?

3. What is the first sign that he is afraid?
4. Why does he decide to fight the duel with a pistol, even though it is more dangerous than a sword?
5. Why was he too afraid to go back to bed?
6. After he has been to see his two seconds, what signs are there that his nervousness is getting worse?
7. In the evening, what does the nobleman say which must have made Signoles even more afraid?
8. What made him certain he was not in a fit state to fight a duel?
9. Why was his last act so foolish?

The Inn

1. Give the names of the two men and the dog who are staying behind to look after the inn.
2. Why do the houses of the village of Leuk look like bits of sand?
3. What evidence is there to suggest that Ulrich and Louise are in love?
4. After it had snowed for four days and nights, how do we know that the inn was almost covered?
5. How cold was it when Hari set out on his hunting expedition?
6. When Hari did not return, what did Ulrich at first think might have happened to him?
7. What preparations did he make and what did he do before setting out at one o'clock?
8. What gave him the energy to get back to the inn after his night out in the snow?
9. Do you think the strange cry had come from his friend – or was the voice only in his dream?
10. Why did Ulrich never dare to open the door?
11. What suggests that the dog sensed that there was a ghost outside the door?
12. What explanation could you give for the strange sounds which came from outside?
13. Why did old Hauser at first think that all was well in the inn?
14. How did they know that Ulrich was mad, even before the doctors told them?

The Necklace

1. Why was Mrs Loisel not pleased to receive the invitation?
2. What sacrifice did her husband make?
3. How do we know that Mrs Forester was rich?
4. What suggests that the women enjoyed the party far more than the men?
5. Describe the efforts they make to find the missing necklace.
6. What kind of things did Mrs Loisel have to do now that they were poor?
7. Why did Mrs Forester not recognise her?
8. This is one of Maupassant's best known stories, mainly because of the 'surprise ending'. Did it surprise you?

A Vendetta

1. What did Mother Saverini mean when she promised her dead son 'a vendetta'?
2. Why would she have to perform the vendetta herself?
3. How did the dog behave when it was given no food?
4. Why did Mother Saverini thread the sausage so that it went inside the dummy's neck?
5. Why did she train the dog to attack the dummy when there was no food there?
6. Why did the old woman sleep well that night?

The Unknown

1. What was so unusual about the sight of the two beggars round a fire?
2. When do people become afraid, according to the man on the train?
3. Why did Turgenev get such a shock when he felt the hand on his shoulder?
4. Name at least four things during the walk in Finistère which made the story-teller so afraid.
5. Why did he not realise that the cart was being pushed by a child?

A Nightmare in Paris

1. What suggests that the writer is very strange?
2. Give three reasons why it became impossible for him to tell what time it was.
3. Do you think this really was a nightmare – or do you think this story was told by a madman?

Coco

1. How do we know that the farmer was a wealthy man?
2. Explain carefully why the boy hated the old horse.
3. Why did the horse get so hungry when it was in the field?
4. What made the horse suffer even more?
5. Do you agree that this story might help to stop cruelty to animals?

He?

1. This story is in the form of a letter to a friend. Why was the letter written?
2. What things make the writer so afraid?
3. Why does he decide to go out one damp evening in autumn?
4. Why does he think the man in the chair must be a friend?
5. Why does he hide the chair behind the bed?
6. When the writer says that he knows the ghost doesn't exist, do you think he is sure?
7. What is your own explanation for this strange experience?

A Duel

1. Why was Mr Dubuis making this train journey?
2. Give examples of the way the Prussian officer boasts.
3. How does he first insult Mr Dubuis?

4. Why does Mr Dubuis find it easy to attack the Prussian on the train?
5. Give two reasons why Mr Dubuis is amazed to see the Prussian fall flat on his face.
6. What things does this French writer suggest about the character of Englishmen?

Who Knows?

1. Why has the writer become so fond of the objects in his house?
2. When he returns home after the theatre, why is it strange that he starts to feel nervous?
3. Why does he say he knew his revolver was useless?
4. Why does he suddenly find the courage to rush forward to stop the desk?
5. Why do you think the doctors advised the writer to travel?
6. What does he notice about the street in Rouen which makes it seem mysterious?
7. What makes the antique dealer seem so mysterious and evil?
8. Why do you think the police officer looks at the writer rather suspiciously?
9. How does Philippe think that the furniture has been returned to the house?
10. Why is the writer so afraid of the antique dealer?
11. Why does he not want any visitors?
12. Do you think that the story-teller really is mad? Give reasons for your decision.

OXFORD PROGRESSIVE ENGLISH READERS

GRADE 1

Vocabulary restricted to 1900 head words
Illustrated partly in two and partly in full colours
One illustration every 6 pages on average

The Adventures of Hang Tuah	MUBIN SHEPPARD
Alice's Adventures in Wonderland	LEWIS CARROLL
A Christmas Carol	CHARLES DICKENS
Don Quixote	CERVANTES
Great Expectations	CHARLES DICKENS
Gulliver's Travels	JONATHAN SWIFT
Jane Eyre	CHARLOTTE BRONTË
Little Women	LOUISA M. ALCOTT
Oliver Twist	CHARLES DICKENS
Plays for Malaysian Schools I	PATRICK YEOH
The Stone Junk	RETOLD BY D.H. HOWE
Stories of Shakespeare's Plays I	RETOLD BY N. KATES
The Tale of the Bounty	RETOLD BY H.G. WYATT
Tales from Tolstoy	RETOLD BY R.D. BINFIELD
Tales of Si Kabayan	MURTAGH MURPHY
The Talking Tree & Other Stories	DAVID McROBBIE
The Tiger of Lembah Pahit	NORMA R. YOUNGBERG
A Time of Darkness	SHAMUS FRAZER
Treasure Island	R.L. STEVENSON

GRADE 2

Vocabulary restricted to 2900 head words
One two-coloured illustration every 10 pages on average

Around the World in Eighty Days	JULES VERNE
Asia Pacific Stories	MURTAGH MURPHY
Beau Geste	P.C. WREN
Chinese Tales of the Supernatural	RETOLD BY BENJAMIN CHIA
The Crocodile Dies Twice	SHAMUS FRAZER
David Copperfield	CHARLES DICKENS
Five Tales	OSCAR WILDE
Hound of the Baskervilles	SIR ARTHUR CONAN DOYLE
Journey to the Centre of the Earth	JULES VERNE
The Missing Scientist	S.F. STEVENS
Plays for Malaysian Schools II	PATRICK YEOH
Robinson Crusoe	DANIEL DEFOE
Seven Chinese Stories	T.J. SHERIDAN
Stories of Shakespeare's Plays II	RETOLD BY WYATT & FULLERTON
A Tale of Two Cities	CHARLES DICKENS
Tales of Crime & Detection	RETOLD BY G.F. WEAR
Two Famous English Comedies	RETOLD BY RICHARD CROFT
Vanity Fair	W.M. THACKERAY

GRADE 3

Vocabulary restricted to 3500 head words
One two-coloured illustration every 15 pages on average

The Gifts & Other Stories	O. HENRY & OTHERS
Kidnapped	R.L. STEVENSON
King Solomon's Mines	RIDER HAGGARD
Lady Precious Stream	S.I. HSIUNG
The Moonstone	WILKIE COLLINS
A Night of Terror & Other Strange Tales	GUY DE MAUPASSANT
The Red Winds	SHAMUS FRAZER
Seven Stories	H.G. WELLS
Stories of Shakespeare's Plays III	RETOLD BY H.G. WYATT
Tales of Mystery & Imagination	EDGAR ALLAN POE
20,000 Leagues under the Sea	JULES VERNE
The War of the Worlds	H.G. WELLS
Wuthering Heights	EMILY BRONTË